"He said to get out while I could... if I wanted to live."

Nick choked, sputtering his soft drink over the table. He grabbed a napkin to clean up the mess he'd made, stunned at what he'd heard. "He said *what*?"

Macy repeated the threat, looking lost, while Nick stared at her. What was going on here? Someone threatened to kill her if she stayed in this house. So what was hidden here that someone wanted bad enough to pull something like this? Or was it someone who wanted to get her out of town before she found out something better left secret?

He wanted to reach across the table and take her hand, tell her it would be all right, but she'd know he was lying. Nothing would be all right until they found out the truth about Megan Douglas's death and learned for certain who had killed her. Most important, he had to find the jerk harassing Macy before this situation turned deadly.

Barbara Warren started making up stories when she was young. When she grew older, she began working on her dream of becoming a real writer. Now writing is an important part of her life and she tries to make time for it almost every day. Barbara lives in the rural Ozarks with her husband. You can learn more about her at her website, barbarawarrenbluemountainedit.com, or on Facebook.

Books by Barbara Warren

Love Inspired Suspense

Dangerous Inheritance

DANGEROUS INHERITANCE

BARBARA WARREN

HARLEQUIN® LOVE INSPIRED® SUSPENSE

Recycling programs
for this product may
not exist in your area.

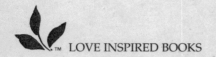

LOVE INSPIRED BOOKS

ISBN-13: 978-0-373-44659-9

Dangerous Inheritance

Copyright © 2015 by Barbara Warren

All rights reserved. Except for use in any review, the reproduction
or utilization of this work in whole or in part in any form by any
electronic, mechanical or other means, now known or hereinafter
invented, including xerography, photocopying and recording, or in
any information storage or retrieval system, is forbidden without
the written permission of the editorial office, Love Inspired Books,
233 Broadway, New York, NY 10279 U.S.A.

This is a work of fiction. Names, characters, places and incidents are
either the product of the author's imagination or are used fictitiously, and
any resemblance to actual persons, living or dead, business establishments,
events or locales is entirely coincidental.

This edition published by arrangement with Love Inspired Books.

® and TM are trademarks of Love Inspired Books, used under license.
Trademarks indicated with ® are registered in the United States Patent
and Trademark Office, the Canadian Intellectual Property Office and in
other countries.

www.Harlequin.com

Printed in U.S.A.

Though I walk in the midst of trouble,
Thou wilt revive me: Thou shalt stretch forth Thine hand
against the wrath of mine enemies,
and Thy right hand shall save me.
–Psalms 138:7

Dedicated to Mary Lowe, Carol Parscale, Randi Perry,
Ronica Stramel and Alice Leverich, my critique group,
and to my agent, Terry Burns, who works so hard for me.
And a special thank-you to Tina James and Emily Krupin
at Love Inspired Suspense for being so helpful
and so easy to work with. I appreciate you very much.

ONE

A car drove by and turned the corner, but Macy Douglas ignored it. All her attention was centered on her grandmother Lassiter's house—the house where her mother had been brutally murdered—the house where her father had been arrested as the killer. The house she couldn't remember, even though she had apparently lived here the first seven years of her life. Dark and forbidding, and at least two stories tall, it sat back from the street on a large lot. She hadn't realized the house would be this big—or this intimidating.

Lightning flared. A gust of wind rattled the branches overhead like dry bones. She shot a glance upward before giving herself a mental shake. Enough of this. She had to stop being such a coward. It was just a house, the house a grandmother she couldn't remember had left to her.

It was hers…and she didn't want it.

Didn't want the secrets hiding behind that innocent-looking facade. Secrets better left dormant behind the barrier her mind had erected, protecting her from the horror of that night.

She stared up at the rounded turret of the old Queen

Anne house. What had really happened here? In spite of her resolve to learn the truth, did she really want to know? Would the knowledge destroy all she wanted to believe about her father?

When Grandmother Douglas lay dying she had gasped out "the box." When Macy found the metal box with information about her father's death in prison, there had also been a letter telling her not to come here, that it would be dangerous. But she had come because she needed to know the truth about her family—the truth about what had happened in this house.

Lightning flashed again, illuminating the wide porch and the front of the house. Thunder grumbled overhead.

Macy climbed the steps and inserted the key her grandmother Lassiter's lawyer had sent her. The door swung open, silent as a shadow. She caught her breath, listening, but the low growl of thunder and the wind whipping the tree limbs were the only sounds. She fumbled for the light switch.

A chandelier sprang to life and she had a fleeting impression of a mahogany table, the glint of a gold framed mirror, before a jagged spear of lightning split the sky.

Thunder exploded.

The lights went out!

Darkness closed around her, the silence like a heavy blanket. Macy glanced behind her. The streetlight on the corner shed a circle of dull light, but all the houses in the area were dark. The lightning must have done major damage. She turned back to face the house, fumbling in her pocket for the penlight she carried. Her fingers closed around the smooth cylinder. The tiny light barely dented the darkness. A staircase rose on the left, disappearing into the ebony depths of the upper regions.

A door beckoned, and Macy crept toward it. She caught a glimpse of old-fashioned chairs and a fireplace.

A slight movement at the window suddenly caught her attention. A pale oval pressed against the glass—someone was peering in.

Watching her.

Macy whirled, running to the door. She plunged down the porch steps and strode around the house, swinging the penlight from side to side. Right there. That's where the sneak had to have been standing. So where was he now?

Then strong arms clamped around her, yanking her back in a tight embrace. Macy dropped the penlight. A scream ripped from her throat as she clawed at the arms encircling her, trying to break loose.

Nick Baldwin grunted and caught the intruder's shoulders, swinging the guy around. The stranger's ball cap fell off and long copper-colored hair swung down, swirling in the wind. Nick revised his impression in a hurry. This was no man.

It was a woman! A very angry woman determined to break his hold, and he had his hands full trying to stop her.

"Let *go* of me." She twisted her body, trying to wrench loose.

His grip tightened. "Whoa! Take it easy. I'm not going to hurt you."

He propelled her toward the front porch and jerked out his cell phone. "Sit down on that step so I can keep an eye on you."

She sat, glaring up at him, and he had the impression she was braced to jump and run. A jagged flash of lightning slashed the sky, followed by a cannon blast of thunder. The storm was moving closer.

He ended the call and stood in front of her, firm and unyielding. "You just sit there for a few minutes. I've got someone coming to help straighten this out."

She arched an eyebrow. "You can't handle one woman by yourself?"

Amused by her question, he chuckled, breaking the tension. There was laughter in his voice when he spoke. "I don't think that's the problem. I'm Nick Baldwin, a police officer here in Walnut Grove. And right now— like it or not—I'm in charge. You just sit there for the time being and we'll try to get everything worked out before the storm hits."

A sprinkle of raindrops greeted his words, and the woman glanced at the sky, looking startled. He hoped it wouldn't start pouring, but if it did, they could move to the wide front porch.

He stood before her, relaxed, but blocking her from leaving. Nick was aware that with his back to the street his face was hidden in the shadows, so she would have no idea what he looked like. But the dim glow from the streetlight had to show her he was in uniform. A policeman.

She stared up at him. "Why were you looking in the window?"

"I saw a light moving around in the house and then you came barreling out. I've got some questions for you, but they can wait for a few minutes."

A police car pulled into the driveway and parked behind her Chevy. Sam Halston got out and left the motor running and the lights on, illuminating the scene.

"Hey, Nick. What've we got here?"

Nick turned to face him. "I saw something like a flashlight in a house that's supposed to be locked and unoccupied, and then she came rushing out the door and down the steps like something was chasing her. Thought it might be a good idea to check her out. I'd be interested in learning how she got inside and what she was doing there."

Sam approached. "Okay, let's see what's going on. You got any identification?"

The woman switched her attention to him, but she didn't look any friendlier. "It's in the car. If you can call off your watchdog, I'll go get it."

"Well, now, I think it might be better if Nick escorted you. We can't take a chance on you hopping in and driving off, now can we?"

She didn't answer, but she got to her feet and marched down the drive. Nick followed her, watching as she reached inside the car and retrieved her purse. She took out her driver's license and handed it to him, but he could tell from her expression she was ticked off.

He tilted the license to the light, then glanced in her direction. "Macy Douglas. You're not from here, so what are you doing in Opal Lassiter's house?"

"She was my grandmother."

Sam stepped forward. "Let me see that."

He took her license from Nick. "So, you're Steve Douglas's daughter. I heard you might be coming to town. How long are you here for?"

"I have no idea. Does it matter?" A gust of wind lashed the branches of the trees and whipped her long copper-colored hair into her eyes. She sent a quick glance overhead at the approaching storm.

He handed back the license. "I'm Sam Halston, chief of police in Walnut Grove."

Nick glanced at him through narrowed eyes. So Sam was familiar with her name. And how had he heard she might be coming to town? It was time he took part in the conversation. "We've had a problem with attempted break-ins at this house recently. So far, whoever it was got scared off before getting in, and the neighborhood watch in this area is used to being on guard. They kept an eye on Opal while she lived here."

"Are you saying someone reported me when I drove in? How did you get here so fast? I'd only been in the house for a few minutes before you showed up."

He could hear the suspicion in her voice. Well, that worked both ways. He was a little suspicious himself and he hadn't learned yet why she was in the house. "I've made a habit of driving by and keeping an eye on things, and it's a small town. It doesn't take long to get to any part of it. But none of this answers the most important question. Why are you here at this time of the night?"

She hesitated, and he waited, his eyes holding hers. Finally she sighed and started talking. "This house is a piece of my family history, and I was curious about it. I suppose I could have waited until morning, but I wanted to find it and see what it looked like."

"You lived here when you were young," Sam said. "You ought to have some memories of it."

"I was seven years old when I left, and no, I don't remember much." She slid her license into her wallet and closed her purse, slinging it over her shoulder. "May I go now?"

"That depends," Sam said, sounding reluctant. "Where are you going?"

"To a motel, I guess. If there's one in town that still has lights."

"There's a good one on the highway, and the outage is just on this side of town. It'll probably be off for several hours. Nick'll show you how to find the motel, and I want to have a talk with you in the morning."

Macy shook her head. "I have a nine o'clock appointment with Raleigh Benson, my grandmother's lawyer."

"Make it eight, then. Nick will give you directions." He turned and walked away. A handful of raindrops splattered around them and Nick motioned toward her car.

"We'd better get. It's going to start pouring in a few minutes. I'm parked just around the corner. Follow me, and I'll show you the way to the motel."

"First I have to lock the house."

They hurried back to the porch and he waited while she climbed the steps, checked the light switch and locked the door before jogging over to their separate cars.

Nick walked around the corner to his car and drove back to the driveway, pulling in front of Macy to lead the way. He watched in his rearview mirror, making sure she followed him. She hadn't been all that cooperative, and he wouldn't put it past her to speed off in the other direction.

Of course, the way he'd surprised her might have something to do with how she'd acted. The minute he'd felt the softness of her shoulders, seen the glimmer of that long hair flashing across her face, he knew he'd messed up. Even in the pale glow of the streetlight, that copper-colored hair held a fire of its own. A man could warm his hands by it.

Since she was from out of town the possibilities of her being their mystery burglar were practically nonexistent. But why didn't she remember living here? After all, she'd spent a few years in this house. She should remember something. But what was she doing here, alone, at this time of night? Her explanation had been lame, to put it mildly. And what was she doing inside the house?

Macy Douglas still had some explaining to do.

Macy followed him into the parking lot of a Motel 6, the windshield wipers slapping at a barrage of raindrops. Nick got out and hurried toward her car, shoulders hunched and head ducked against the wind. She rolled down the window and he stuck his head inside, the rain pelting his shoulders.

She stared at him, looking startled as their eyes met— and held. His heartbeat kicked up a notch. A reaction he hadn't expected and definitely didn't want. Macy leaned back as if trying to put a little distance between them. Maybe he needed to try that, too. Regardless of how lovely she was, he didn't need any more complications in his life.

She seemed almost as surprised as he was. After a split-second hesitation, he said, "You'll be all right here. I'll drop by in the morning and show you the way to the police station. Be ready about seven thirty and we'll pick up a bite to eat first. There's a restaurant in town that puts out a good breakfast."

"That will be fine, I guess," she muttered.

He nodded and stepped back. "I'll go with you to check in and get your room number."

They hurried toward the office, Nick striding along with her. She probably didn't want to check in with a policeman standing beside her. He could understand that. It wasn't the best way to make a good impression.

The motel clerk eyed them curiously, but he assigned her a room and handed her a key. Nick lifted her suitcase out of the car. A curtain of rain danced on the pavement and bounced off the motel roof, soaking them both. She unlocked the door and turned to face him. Crystal raindrops glistened in her hair, and those sea-green eyes fringed with thick dark lashes seemed to warm for a moment.

She smiled suddenly and his heartbeat kicked up another notch. "Thank you for showing me the way to the motel. I'd probably still be driving around, lost in a strange town. Now you'd better get in out of the rain."

He nodded and handed her a card. "You need anything, call me. I'll see you in the morning."

He noticed she watched him run back to his patrol car before going inside and locking the door.

Nick drove away from the motel thinking about Macy Douglas. The sudden flare of attraction he'd felt that moment in the motel parking lot had surprised him, but he couldn't deny there had been a spark between them. The way she had stood up to him and to Sam, not giving an inch, was impressive. He'd give her one thing, she was a fighter. And she had the kind of beauty that would be hard for any man to resist.

He'd known her grandmother Lassiter, and everyone in town knew about the brutal murder of Opal's daughter, Megan Douglas, and that Steve, Megan's husband, had been convicted of killing her and had died in prison. It was part of the town's history. A part most of them would just as soon forget.

He drew up to a stoplight, his thoughts still on Macy.

Opal had led a quiet life, not getting involved in community affairs, but he had a hunch her granddaughter would be different. Yet he sensed vulnerability behind that feisty behavior, as if she were afraid of something. Maybe he could find out more tomorrow at breakfast.

Nick hurried home to change into dry clothes and then drove to the police station. Sam greeted him as he entered. "You get the Douglas woman settled all right?"

"She's at Motel 6. Or at least that's where I left her. Why? What's up?"

"I'm wondering why she came to town, and why now. She hasn't been back since she was a kid, and I've got a hunch she's up to something. You're too young to remember what it was like when Megan Douglas was killed. She was well liked, went to church, owned and ran her own business. Steve was something else."

"How so?"

Sam leaned back in his chair, getting comfortable. "Steve had a favorite in the state senate race, and it wasn't our Garth Nixon. Steve went all out, using his newspaper to influence the voters in this area. Pretty much divided the town—even divided the whole district. Cost Garth the election. I'd hate to see it all stirred up again. You never know how people will react, and if she's anything like her dad, things could get out of hand."

"What does that have to do with his wife's death?"

"The police chief was Garth's cousin. When Steve was arrested, some people figured it was payback time, like maybe the police didn't try hard enough to find the real killer."

Nick stared at Sam, thinking about what he had just said. The police had been accused of playing dirty? His father had been a cop back then. No way would his dad have been a part of anything like that—not the man he remembered and had looked up to. "You can't be serious. My dad was an honest cop. He'd have quit before he stood by and let someone pull something wrong. You know better than that."

Sam shrugged. "I'm guessing there could have been some dirty work going on. There's always that possibility. And no, I don't think your dad would have taken part, but he might not have known about it. I don't know all that much about what went on, and at the time it wasn't any of my business, so I really didn't care all that much."

Nick narrowed his eyes. "That was what, twelve or thirteen years ago?"

"More like seventeen, I believe. Macy was just a kid. He knocked her out, almost killed her. And that was another problem. Regardless of Steve's politics, a lot of people had trouble believing he'd kill his wife or hurt his own kid. He was crazy about that girl."

Nick remembered the way Macy Douglas had stared at the old house. Something had brought her to Walnut Grove and he had a feeling it was rooted in the past.

"If he was innocent, that means there might still be a killer out there who doesn't want to get caught."

TWO

Morning light filtered through the blinds as Macy glanced around the motel room. This wasn't turning out to be a great day. First she needed to get through the meeting with Sam Halston. Then she had the meeting with the lawyer, another thing she wasn't looking forward to. According to him, her grandmother Lassiter had been dead for several months, but he'd had to close out the estate and then it took a while to locate her. And then after seeing the lawyer she would move into her grandmother's house. She had no idea what she was getting into, but there were only two options: carry this through or turn tail and run.

She had no place to run.

When Grandma Mattie had been battling the cancer that had finally killed her, Macy had to take several days off work at Wesley Manufacturing, which hadn't sat well with her supervisor, Lena Hankins, a cold, play-it-by-the-book woman who didn't believe in second chances. Then when she had needed a few days to get her grandmother's affairs in order Lena had given her a choice: forget it or quit.

Fresh from the funeral and still wounded by losing

the only family member she had left, Macy had walked out. So here she was, no job, no family, no one who cared. She'd listed Grandma Mattie's house for sale, but so far, no takers.

And eating breakfast with Nick Baldwin seemed way too intimate. What had she been thinking? A knock on the door sent her hurrying to open it. Nick stood there in his police uniform, the rising sun dusting his shoulders with gold. His smile was warm and welcoming. At this stage in her life, warm and welcoming was good. He was also six feet or more of muscle and charm. A deadly combination.

His dark hair was combed back, not rumpled as it had been in last night's storm, and his golden-brown eyes were friendly as he stepped back to let her walk past. She accidently brushed against him, and quickly moved on, more aware of him than she liked. What was it about Nick Baldwin that affected her this way?

He smiled and her pulse rate accelerated. "I guess we'd better go in separate cars since you have an appointment with your lawyer right after you talk to Sam."

The flare of disappointment caught her by surprise. After all, it wasn't as if she wanted to spend more time with him—or did she?

And her lawyer? She'd never met Raleigh Benson. Would he be friendly to the granddaughter who had never seen or talked to Opal Lassiter, her maternal grandmother, in the past seventeen years? Or would he be one of the enemies her grandmother Douglas had warned her about in the letter Macy had found after her death?

Macy closed the door and locked it behind her, and they walked through the parking area. The April air smelled fresh and clean after the rain. A sprinkling of new leaves brightened the tall oaks, and sturdy green shoots of jonquils held a promise of golden blooms to come. Nick waved from his car and she followed, finding it hard to believe that she was actually looking forward to having breakfast with him.

Last night she had been ready to deck him. Had her feelings toward him changed that fast? Grandma Mattie had believed the police in Walnut Grove were corrupt. What about Nick? Could she trust him, or beneath that friendliness was he really her enemy?

She drove into the restaurant lot and found a spot to park close to his car. He stood beside it waiting for her. Today he bore little resemblance to the hard, suspicious policeman he'd been last night. Tall, broad shoulders filling his uniform, he had the kind of rugged good looks she liked in a man. His grin lit up his face.

Her lips moved in an answering smile that was a little more spontaneous than she intended. She jerked herself up short, clamping down on her emotions. No matter how good-looking Nick Baldwin was, the last thing she needed was to get involved with a policeman. At least not until she learned more about this town…and Nick.

Nick held the restaurant door open for Macy, noticing the way the sun struck glowing bronze highlights in her hair. She was even more beautiful than he'd realized, and she wasn't angry or nervous the way she'd been last night. Maybe it had just been stress from driving in an unfamiliar place after dark with a storm threatening, and then being harassed by a stranger.

He reached for a menu, wondering why she was here. He didn't know anything about this woman, but for some reason he was interested in her, and it had nothing to do with the way she looked, or that vulnerable expression she wore some of the time. Or at least that's what he wanted to believe.

As a matter of fact, he really couldn't explain why he spent so much time thinking about her. Maybe he should back off a little until he found out more about what was going on. He needed to remain professional, concentrate on her reason for being here, instead of thinking of her as a woman who needed his help.

The waitress took their order: eggs and sausage for him, cheese omelet and a cup of peach yogurt for her. Nick smiled in approval. He liked a woman with a good appetite. He leaned back and studied Macy. She had the same copper-colored hair and green eyes as her deceased mother, judging from the pictures he'd found of Megan Douglas in his research last night on the internet. There hadn't been much, just a couple of articles about the trial. Not a lot of help.

But regardless of how good she looked, he couldn't let those sea-green eyes and that dusting of freckles across her nose distract him from the job at hand—learning why Macy Douglas was in Walnut Grove and what she hoped to accomplish. He didn't believe she just decided all at once to visit. Something had brought her here, and he wanted to know what. He had a personal interest in this now since his father might have had a hand in sending her dad to prison.

Before he could speak, she put down her fork and gave him a straight look. "Tell me the truth—how did you manage to get to that house so fast last night? I'd only been there for a few minutes before you grabbed me. And why were you parked around the corner instead of in the driveway?"

So all right, maybe she wasn't as calm as she appeared to be, and apparently she hadn't forgiven him for his part in what had happened. He searched for the right words. Until he knew why she was here, he wasn't about to discuss police business with her.

"Like I said, I got a call that you'd pulled into the drive and I was nearby. I drove past just as you stopped. Since I didn't know who you were or why you were there, I just went around the block and parked, then walked the rest of the way."

She looked thoughtful. "I see. You said there had been attempted break-ins. What were they looking for, and why didn't they succeed?"

He took a sip of coffee so hot it burned his tongue, trying to decide how to answer. "I don't know what they're looking for. As for why they didn't succeed, people were used to watching to see if Opal was all right or if she needed anything."

She gave him a skeptical glance. "Go on."

He shrugged, hoping to appease her without giving away too much. "Opal had an alarm system installed a couple of years ago. That went off once recently, scaring the burglar away and alerting her neighbors. And people are quick to call in if they see anything suspicious. It's a good neighborhood. They watch out for each other."

Whoever was trying to break in had damaged the alarm system so it didn't work anymore, which was one reason the police were keeping an eye on the place, and why the neighbors were on high alert. Someone was determined to get inside Opal Lassiter's house. It was common knowledge she didn't keep anything of value at home, so there had to be another reason for the recent attempts to break in, and he wondered whether it might tie into the sudden appearance of Macy Douglas. Like the robber knew she was coming and wanted to find something before she got there.

He wondered how many people had expected Macy Douglas to show up in town. Sam knew. So how did he find out?

Macy picked up her glass of water and sipped. "Too bad they didn't have a system like that in place when my mother was killed."

Nick caught the bitterness in her voice and understood it completely. Compassion surged through him for this woman who had lost so much. "Things are different today, I guess. More people, more crime. But the police were convinced they had the killer. There was evidence to back up that decision."

Macy gave him a stern look, as if daring him to dispute her words. "The police were wrong. My father wasn't a killer. He was a good, decent man who was sent to prison for a crime he didn't commit. And he died there."

Nick stared at her, caught by the conviction in her voice. So that was what she believed. Maybe Sam was right. Her coming could stir up trouble they might not be able to control. Start talk like that and people would line up taking sides.

"Do you have any proof of what you're saying?"

"No, but I'm going to find it, even if I have to turn this town on its ear."

Judging from the green fire burning in her eyes, he figured she just might do that. According to Sam, passions still ran high over what had happened back then, but most of what he'd heard had been about the election. A woman had been killed. Surely that should have been everyone's first concern. Had the murder of Megan Douglas gotten lost in the uproar over a failed election? Some people seemed to lose what little sense they had when it came to politics.

Nick glanced at his watch, hating to end this conversation, but they had to go.

"Are you through? If you are, we need to leave. It's almost time for you to meet with Sam."

He dropped some bills on the table, enough to pay for breakfast and provide a tip, and followed her outside. "I'll lead the way. It's just a short distance from here."

Macy didn't look happy, but she nodded and got in her car, and he did the same.

He wasn't sure what Sam had in mind, but whatever it was, he intended to keep an eye on Macy Douglas. Judging from the mood she was in, there was no telling what kind of trouble she might stir up.

Nick parked in front of the police station and waited for Macy to join him. Their conversation in the restaurant had been puzzling. He guessed it was normal for her to hope her father wasn't guilty, but she had sounded so sure. Did she have evidence of some kind that led her to believe in his innocence? If she did, where had she found it, and why had it surfaced after all these years?

They entered the building, and Nick led her into the police chief's office and at Sam's instruction, took a chair against the wall.

Macy sat down across the desk from Sam, looking a little intimidated. Most people felt nervous at being summoned to a police station, whether or not they had done anything wrong. And here he was sitting behind her, as if he was blocking her from leaving. He guessed he could understand how she felt.

Sam leaned forward, resting his arms on the desktop. Medium height, carrying about ten pounds more than he needed, and his hair thinning on top, he didn't look as intimidating as he had last night. Nick hoped that would help Macy relax.

The police chief eyed her intently. "You had a rough welcome to Walnut Grove. I hope it goes better from here on out."

"Thank you."

He waited, staring at her as if he wanted more. "How long are you planning to stay?"

Nick had a hunch she probably didn't want to answer Sam's question.

"I'm not sure. I haven't talked to my grandmother's lawyer yet, and I haven't had a chance to inspect the house. Depending on what I learn, I might be here for an extended visit."

Sam nodded, his expression and tone of voice sending a clear message that he wasn't happy with her answer, or with her presence in Walnut Grove. "What do you know about your mother's death?"

Macy looked like she didn't want to answer that, either, and Nick wanted to jump in and ask a few questions of his own, but this was Sam's show, so he made an effort to keep quiet.

After taking a deep breath, she said, "Just that she was murdered in that house. I was very young and my grandmother Douglas never talked about it, but she was convinced my father was innocent."

Sam pressed his lips together as if she had just confirmed what he suspected. When he spoke, his voice was stern, almost condemning. "This is a quiet little place. Oh, we have crime, but nothing like murder, as a general rule. What happened hurt the town and I'd hate to see it all stirred up again."

Macy bristled as if she was getting a little of her spunk back. "I believe it hurt my family more than it hurt the town. And if stirring things up again—as you put it—can clear my father's name and bring my mother's killer to justice, then that's the way it has to be."

"Your parents are both dead. Nothing you can do now will help them. But ripping this town apart over something that happened years ago can do a lot of damage. I won't allow that to happen."

She stood, apparently ready to leave whether he liked it or not. "I have no intention of damaging anything or anyone, but I *will* do everything in my power to find out what happened to my family and who was responsible. I'll be living in my grandmother's house until I learn the truth."

Sam shoved his chair back and got to his feet. "You may be putting yourself in danger. Have you thought of that?"

"Of course I've thought about it, and since you've made it clear I can't expect any help from the police, it looks like I'm on my own."

She gripped the back of the chair. "Let me ask you something. You say someone is trying to break into my grandmother's house. What do you think they hope to find? And what do you plan to do about it?"

She whirled and stalked out before he could answer, not even glancing at Nick to see how he took her confrontation with his boss.

He watched Macy stride from the room before glancing across the desk at Sam. "What was that all about?"

Sam shrugged. "That woman is trouble. The sooner she leaves town, the better."

"If she owns a house in Walnut Grove, I'd say she has a right to be here."

"She's up to something and I don't want this department mixed up in it. You stay away from everything connected to Macy Douglas if you know what's good for you."

He walked out of the office, leaving Nick to stare after him. He had to be kidding.

First Sam hinted the police might have been involved in something dirty back when Megan Douglas was murdered. Then he ordered him to just drop it, stay away from the woman who was stirring things up? Regardless of how Sam felt, Nick would keep an eye on Macy Douglas. Someone had to, and it looked like it was up to him.

THREE

Macy drove to the motel, paid her bill and loaded her suitcase in the car. The meeting with the attorney had just been more of the same behavior she'd experienced from Sam Halston—she needed to sell the house and leave town.

She'd learned a couple of things, though. Her grandmother hadn't left her the house. Her parents had left it to her. Opal Lassiter moved into the house where her daughter had died when her own husband, distraught over Megan's death, committed suicide and left her bankrupt. Apparently she'd done well because she'd left Macy a good-size sum of money. Something she could definitely use. According to the attorney Opal had worked in the bank, she'd moved up to a good position and she had been thrifty. She'd also been a quiet woman, keeping to herself a lot of the time. Church and friends had been her only social activities.

Raleigh Benson had given Macy all the keys to the house he had in his file. She already had one to the front door, but she didn't want other keys out there for someone else to use. Another thing bothered her. Why would a grandmother who made no effort to stay in touch be so generous at her death? It didn't make sense.

She reached the house without any trouble but found Nick Baldwin and his police car parked in her driveway. What was he doing here? Did he intend to stop her from moving in? There must be something in that house they didn't want her to see. Well, she'd find it in spite of them. She might be outnumbered, but she wouldn't give up without a fight.

Macy got out of the car and waited for Nick to join her. Had Sam sent him to check on her? She wouldn't put it past him.

"What are you doing here?"

The smile stayed in place, but there was something watchful about his eyes. "I thought you might need some help moving in."

"I don't have all that much and I can manage just fine." He had to have a reason for showing up at just the right time to help. No, not just showing up. He was waiting for her. Which made her a little uneasy, considering the way she'd already been treated that day.

He shrugged, still looking pleasant. "I thought you might feel more comfortable if you had someone with you when you went inside. I won't get in your way, just be along to keep you company in case you need anything."

And she was supposed to believe this? "Does Sam know you're here?"

The grin faded, but if she'd struck a nerve it didn't show. He shook his head. "No, this is something I'm doing on my own. I just thought it might help if you didn't have to do this alone."

Okay, she hated to admit it, and wasn't going to admit

it to him, but she had been dreading going inside again. Afraid of what she might find or how she would feel. It would be easier to have someone with her, and it was nice of him to think of it—if he was telling the truth. And if he wasn't, she'd deal with it later.

Right now she felt better just to have him standing beside her, strong and dependable. Macy shook her head. Dependable? What was she thinking? She didn't know him well enough to be sure of that. She held up the key ring, steeling herself to face the inevitable. "All right, let's go."

The storm had left a scattering of budding leaves and broken twigs covering the walk. They crunched underfoot as she strode toward the house, hearing him stepping along behind her. Seen in daylight, the house was still imposing. Two stories high plus an attic, cream-colored with light blue and beige trim, a wide porch and a corner turret, classic Queen Anne. Beautiful, but not exactly cozy. *Scary* might be a better word. She swallowed the lump in her throat and fumbled with the key ring the lawyer had given her.

Nick reached over and took it from her. "I'd guess this is the one you need." He inserted it in the lock.

Macy motioned for him to go first, not sure she was ready. She followed, nerves prickling. The entry hall had a hardwood floor and a long mahogany table against one wall, with a wide gold-framed mirror hanging behind it, elegant, but cold. Macy walked slowly through to enter the living room. It looked different in the daylight.

Gold brocade armchairs with high backs flanked the fireplace. A crystal chandelier with a cluster of white candle-like lights hung overhead. An alcove held a matching gold sofa with a scattering of ivory and darker gold pillows. The air smelled musty, as if the house hadn't been aired for some time. Judging from the muted rumble of the furnace, the heat was still on.

The furniture wasn't new, so she assumed it had been here when her parents were alive. At least she hoped it had. Maybe it would jog her memory in some way. She moved farther into the room, nerves keyed to the max, almost forgetting to breathe while waiting for something to spark a recollection.

Nothing.

Macy swallowed her disappointment. What had she expected? That everything would immediately fall into place? When had her life ever been that easy? She walked over to stand in front of the white fireplace with a marble mantel holding several pictures of people she probably should know.

She waited for a hint of recognition. Nothing happened. She turned to Nick. "Is one of these my mother? Would you know?"

He gave her a curious look, and pointed to a photograph of a woman laughing at the camera. She had the same red hair as Macy and now that she really looked, there was a resemblance in the planes of her face, the curve of her lips. Not an exact replica, but there could be no denying the similarities.

"You don't know what she looked like?" Nick asked.

She wasn't sure how he would take it or if he would even believe her, but it was time to tell the truth. "I don't remember her. I don't remember my father, either, or even remember living in this house. The first seven years of my life are a total blank."

Macy watched him trying to take this in. It probably sounded like something she'd made up, but let him try living with it, try realizing that a part of him was missing. That he didn't know what exactly, just the gap in his life. See how he felt then.

"You don't remember anything?" he asked, eyebrows raised.

She hadn't expected him to understand, so why was she disappointed by his reaction? Why would she care if he believed her or not? His belief or disbelief had nothing to do with the truth.

"I have dissociative amnesia. According to my doctor it happens when a person blocks out certain information usually caused by stress from something a person has witnessed. My memory begins when I woke up in the hospital with Grandma Mattie sitting by my bedside. I have no recollection of ever being in this house. I'm hoping living here will help restore what I've lost."

If not, at least she would know she'd tried. But if she could recall the events of the night her mother died, perhaps she could remember the face of the killer, and it would not be her father. It would take strong, irrevocable proof to make her believe otherwise.

Nick still looked uncertain, as if not sure what to think about everything she'd just said. "Let me get this straight. You don't remember anything about living in this house. You don't even remember your parents? Is that what you're saying?"

She gave the collection of photos on the mantel a second look before answering. "That's right. I don't remember anything about them. And I don't remember the grandmother who lived here. She was never a part of my life after I moved to Oklahoma. I didn't know anything about her until I got a call from her lawyer."

He nodded, as if in some way he understood, but he

couldn't. Not really. No one could unless they had lived it. She barely even understood it herself. But according to what she'd learned, she'd been born here, had lived here with her parents the first seven years of her life. Been attacked and left for dead the night her mother was murdered. Add that to the fact that all memories of her parents were gone, as if they had never existed. Then tell her she had no right to dig around in the past. She had every right, whether Sam Halston and Raleigh Benson liked it or not.

Or Nick Baldwin, either, for that matter.

Macy reached for the picture of her mother, and something rustled at the back of her mind. Laughter, soft arms holding her close. Almost as soon as the image came, it vanished, leaving her aching for more.

Her *mother*.

She wanted her mother.

The house had waited for her, large, empty and filled with secrets. Macy suddenly had an overwhelming desire to leave—get out of this place.

Resolutely, she gripped the mantel with both hands, fighting down the billowing wave of fear threatening to submerge her.

God, where are you? Help me. I can't do this on my own.

Gradually the feelings subsided, leaving her in some semblance of control. She took a couple of shaky steps toward the next room. Nick followed, not saying anything, but she was aware of the way he watched her, as if expecting her to fall apart. Well, she almost had, and she was sure there were other shocks waiting for her in this house. She had to expect that. Would she be strong enough to do this?

Only with Your help, God.

Next was the dining room. A long walnut table surrounded by high-backed wooden chairs caught her eye. A matching sideboard sat along one wall with mounted pictures depicting the four seasons arranged above it. Beautiful furnishings, but nothing here spoke to her. Macy moved on, walking through the downstairs.

She ended up in the entry hall again and turned toward the staircase. Nick stopped her. "From what you've said, you probably don't remember, but you were found here at the foot of the stairs. You'd been knocked unconscious. At first the police thought you were dead, but when they discovered you were breathing they rushed you to the hospital in an ambulance."

Macy grasped the newel post with both hands. She'd been found here? Why couldn't she remember?

"Where was my mother?"

"She was lying in front of the living-room fireplace."

"How did she die?" She forced the words out through lips gone numb with shock.

Nick placed his hand over hers, his expression compassionate. She fought an urge to lean against him, draw courage from him.

"Are you sure you want to know?" he asked.

She drew a harsh breath that was almost a sob. "I have to know. After all these years, I can't just pretend it didn't happen. I need to know everything."

He drew her away from the stairs. "Let's sit down for a minute. This is going to be hard for you."

She let him lead her into the living room and sank into the chair he indicated. He sat across from her, leaning forward, elbows resting on his knees. His gaze locked with hers, and she caught her breath at the concern reflected there.

After a minute he started speaking. "She'd been hit repeatedly with the fireplace poker. They found it beside you, and believe you were struck with it, too."

Macy bowed her head, hands tightly clasped in her lap. Tears pooled in her eyes, and she furiously wiped them away. Beaten to death? Her mother? In this room? And she couldn't remember. Even now, after what he'd said, she had a picture in her mind of what it could have been like, but she knew it wasn't real, just a manufactured image. Not a memory.

Nick caught her hands, holding them in his. "Macy, look at me. It was a long time ago. You were just a child. It has nothing to do with you now."

She raised her head to stare at him, tears blurring her vision. "It has everything to do with me. She was my *mother*. My mother was killed here, and I can't even remember her. It's like I've betrayed her in some way. Betrayed them both. My father died in prison and I can't give the police the name of the person who destroyed my parents."

Nick knelt beside Macy, aching to help her, and knowing he couldn't. No one could. All he could do was kneel here and watch her suffer. He couldn't share her grief and feelings of guilt, but he could understand her need. Whatever it took, he was going to do everything possible to help her learn the truth—if it was available after all these years. He wanted to take her in his arms and comfort her, but he was a stranger and he was afraid that would upset her even more. Better to wait and just be here if she needed him.

After a long time she raised her head. "I need to go through the rest of the house. Will you go with me?"

"I'll be glad to." He helped her to her feet and continued holding her hand. To reassure her.

They mounted the stairs together, her hand warm in his, and he slanted a sideways glance at her. She'd almost fallen apart in the living room. There might be even more personal reminders up here. He'd need to stay close. Be ready to help.

It must be horrible for her not to remember her parents. He had good memories of growing up, of times spent with his mother, fishing trips with his dad. He was a cop today because he was following in his father's footsteps. He couldn't imagine not remembering them.

He hadn't been completely honest with Macy. Sure he figured she might be nervous about entering the house, but he also intended to do everything he could to prove the police, particularly his father, were innocent of any wrongdoing.

But if she didn't remember the night her mother died, that had to be part of the reason she was here. What if her memories returned? Would she remember the face of who had killed Megan Douglas? The person who had brutally beaten Macy and left her for dead?

If she did remember, would it be Steve Douglas or someone different? Someone who lived in Walnut Grove and didn't want Steve and Megan's daughter staying here, trying to find out what actually happened that night? Someone who would do everything he could to prevent her from remembering? Macy just might be in more danger than he'd realized.

And what was going on with Sam, behaving the way he had? Almost as if he had a reason for not wanting

Macy Douglas to stay here, a strong personal reason. That brought him up short. Sam had lived here all his life. He claimed to have had no interest in the murder, but what if he wasn't telling the truth?

But then again, if Sam had a hand in the cover-up, why would he mention that the police might be involved? Or was he trying to throw suspicion on them to save his own neck? Nick felt ashamed at the thought. Sam was his boss, his friend. He needed to slow down, not jump to conclusions.

The rooms were in order, and apparently nothing caught Macy's attention. He'd worried that she might remember her parents' room, but she didn't seem to see anything familiar. They turned toward the round turret room at the front, across the hall and down from what he took to be the master bedroom.

Macy stopped in the bedroom doorway, stiff and silent, as if she had received a sudden blow. What had she seen? She released his hand and took one step inside the room, looking around, mouth sagging open and eyes wide. He reached for her, knowing something had happened, but she moved away.

It was a child's room, decorated in pink, pale green and white. Nothing looked new, but there was a floral bedspread with matching curtains, a small white wicker rocking chair and a bookcase full of children's books.

Macy crossed to stand in front of them, fingering one after the other. "I know these. I've read every one. They used to be mine."

She strode across the room to a white corner cabinet. The top shelves held an array of figurines, ceramic animals, things that would appeal to a seven-year-old girl. She ignored them, pulling open the door covering the bottom shelves.

Nick watched as she lifted out a large stuffed brown bear with a pink ribbon tied around its neck.

"Toby." Macy snuggled the soft animal against her, cuddling it close. Behind her, Nick stirred restlessly. She turned to face him. "I remember this room. It was mine and I loved it here, and I loved this bear. It was a gift from my father. Oh, Nick, my memory is coming back!"

That's what he was afraid of. Yes, he wanted to help her, but something about all of this was making him uneasy. What if Steve Douglas really was innocent of killing his wife? What if someone here in Walnut Grove knew the truth? That person wouldn't want Macy to re-member what had really happened that night. She walked downstairs, carrying the bear, and he followed, wishing he knew what to do.

First he'd like to get her out of this house. After all, there was someone trying to break in regularly. What if the person succeeded and found Macy here—alone?

"Look, Macy, you can't stay here by yourself. Why don't you spend a few nights at the motel for a while until you get better acquainted with this house and ev-erything?"

"Everything?" She gave him a long, searching glance. "You mean you think I would be safer at the motel? That I'm in danger because I'm the Douglases' daughter, and I'm here. Isn't that right?"

He puffed out a frustrated breath of air. Yeah, that was what he thought, he just didn't want to put it into words, but she wasn't giving him a choice. He didn't have any-thing to base it on, just a growing feeling of something off center. Maybe it was based on Sam's belief that her coming here could stir up trouble.

"I guess so. I'm just not comfortable with you staying here by yourself."

She nodded, looking serious. "I'm not comfortable with it, either. It's like I'm walking a dark road and I don't know what waits around the next curve. But I feel like this is something I have to do and I truly believe God is with me."

Nick could understand that, but he wanted to be here, too. And where did that need to keep her safe come from? He barely knew Macy Douglas, so why was he going all protective over her? He didn't understand it, but he knew it would take everything he had to walk away and leave her alone.

"All right, but I want you to keep my card handy, and you call me the minute anything bothers you. I mean it, Macy. Don't wait to be sure something is wrong. Call."

"I'll be all right. After all, it's just a house. My grandmother Lassiter lived here. I can, too."

The smile she gave him looked like a brave attempt to appear confident, but it didn't fool him a bit. Macy was afraid.

FOUR

Nick left and Macy closed the door and leaned against it. The house felt cold and empty now that he was gone. How long had it been since anyone except her grandmother had worried about her, or shown any concern for her? She wasn't used to this. She wanted to run after him, beg him to stay, but then she drew a deep breath and wandered into the living room, stopping to examine the pictures.

There were no pictures of her father. Maybe not all that unusual, considering that Grandma Mattie Douglas hadn't appeared to have any pictures of her mother. She moved to stand by the window, looking out. Two women, both mothers, each damaged forever by something beyond their control.

The pictures, or rather the ones that were missing, told the story. Her grandmother Lassiter had refused to display the pictures of the man she believed had killed her daughter. Her grandmother Douglas kept only the ones of the son she believed had been wrongly convicted.

Had the two women's grief and anger extended to Macy? Was that why she knew nothing about her mother's family? Never even knew she had a grandmother named

Opal Lassiter? She was just beginning to understand how many lives had been damaged by what happened here.

Now it was up to her to bring it to a close. Would she be up to the job? Did she have a choice? She'd pretty well burned all her bridges.

The doorbell rang, startling Macy. A tall, husky, pleasant-faced woman stood there, smiling. "Macy? I'm Neva Miller. I have a housecleaning business and I cleaned for your mother and for your grandmother. And I remember you from back then. I'd like to speak with you."

Company was the last thing Macy wanted right now, but she didn't like to be rude, either. She smiled, trying to appear welcoming, but how did this woman know she would be here?

"Come on in. The living room is right through here, but I suppose you know that."

Neva laughed. "Yes, there's not much about this house I don't know. I was surprised to hear you'd moved in. I'm sure it has some difficult memories for you."

"I don't remember much about living here. I was young, and from what I've been told, I was seriously injured at the time my mother was killed."

Neva wore her sandy hair cut short and straight, her face was devoid of makeup, and her jeans and long-sleeved green shirt looked loose and comfortable. Now her blue eyes squinted at Macy. "You don't remember what happened that night?"

"No. That's one of the reasons I'm staying here. I'm hoping something will trigger my memory and it will all come back to me."

"I see." Neva looked thoughtful. "Well, you may be

right. But then again, you might be better off if you don't remember."

Macy ignored that remark and glanced at her watch. There had to be a reason for this visit, so she hoped the woman would get to it. She had planned to do some more exploring before dark, and time was slipping by.

Neva must have realized what she was thinking, because she said, "I suppose you wonder why I'm here. I was hoping I could continue taking care of the house for you the way I did for Megan and Opal. I could use the work and it's a big house. If you tried to clean it yourself, let me tell you, it's a never-ending job. I can set whatever schedule works for you. I'm flexible."

"I'm not sure how long I'll be here, and I don't have any long-term plans right now. You wouldn't be interested in taking me on as a client knowing I might eventually leave, would you?"

Neva beamed. "Of course I would. I'll take care of *you* just like I took care of Megan and Opal."

Macy smiled. She knew what Neva meant, and this house would be a chore for her to keep up the way it should be. "All right. What would be a good day for you to come?"

"Any day you like."

Macy thought for a minute. "How about Friday? Would that be convenient?"

Neva agreed, and promised to be there Friday morning around nine o'clock. She coughed suddenly, gasping for breath. "Water."

Macy hurried to the kitchen to drop ice cubes into a glass. She turned on the water, letting it run until it was cold. Neva had stopped coughing, and Macy thought she heard a soft brushing sound from the other room, as if the woman was moving around. But when she carried the glass of water into the living room, Neva was sitting where Macy had left her.

Neva drained half of the liquid before glancing up at Macy. "Thank you, dear. Got a frog in my throat. Allergies. They're bad this time of the year."

Neva left soon after that and Macy locked the door behind her. She stood for a minute, overwhelmed by the heavy silence. Could she stay here? Alone? At night? Pride stiffened her spine. She'd set this course for herself. She couldn't quit now.

She wished she hadn't agreed to let Neva work for her. Looking back she couldn't find a reason for the way she felt. Maybe it was just the fear and suspicion she felt about Walnut Grove and the people who lived here. Another thought occurred to her. How had Neva learned she was here?

Grandma Mattie's letter she'd found in the box of papers containing information about her mother's murder, and her father's conviction and death in prison, had warned against going to Walnut Grove. Things she'd known nothing about. She'd been curious about her parents, asked questions, only to be brushed off by her grandmother, who made it clear she didn't want to talk about the past. After a while Macy had stopped asking.

After Grandma Mattie's funeral, she'd decided to ignore the letter, determined to discover the truth and clear her father's name. But there was one thing she could only ignore at her own peril—since she didn't know who her family's enemy was, she'd be a fool to trust anyone.

Now that Neva had finally left, Macy spent her time prowling through the downstairs rooms. Not looking for anything in particular, just getting acquainted. She was standing in the kitchen when a sound startled her. She held her breath, listening. Had she heard something, or was it just her imagination?

It came again, a distant rattle. Startled, she rushed to the window and identified the source. A garbage truck rumbled up the street. Nothing to be afraid of—nothing but the house. And yes, she was afraid of this house. Afraid of what lay hidden within these walls. The silence smothered her until she longed to get out, get away from the implied threat lurking in the echoing rooms.

It was probably caused by the fact that she felt completely alone, with no one to talk to, no one to rely on. In the months Grandma Mattie had been sick most of her friends had drifted away.

Even Clark, her so-called fiancé, the man she thought cared for her and would stand by her forever, hadn't lasted two months. He'd needed his freedom, claimed he couldn't be tied to a woman who had to spend her time taking care of her sick grandmother. A woman who didn't have enough time for him.

The pain caused by his rejection had been devastating, but it had also taught her two valuable lessons: be careful about trusting anyone, and pretty words didn't mean much without commitment behind them. It had also left her with a firm conviction that most men shouldn't be trusted. She thought of Nick Baldwin. Did that include him? She didn't know yet. He'd have to prove himself before she made that decision.

Macy checked the doors, making sure they were safely locked. She paused at the foot of the stairs, looking up. The rooms above her waited with all the patience of a crouching lion. She climbed slowly, one step at a time, gripping the railing so tightly her hand ached. A step creaked underfoot. The hairs on her arms furred. The house smelled old, abandoned. It needed a good cleaning.

No, it needed people, a family. Would this sad, lonely house ever be a home again?

At the top of the stairs, she walked through the rooms, trying to decide where to sleep. Not in what was obviously the master bedroom—that had surely been her parents' room. She wasn't up to moving in there just yet. Not in the child's room, either. Thinking about it sent a shiver up her back. Why hadn't she been up here where she belonged that night? What had caused her to leave her bed and go downstairs? It was something she had to try to remember, but she couldn't bear the thought of sleeping there. At least not yet.

She also avoided the room that must have been her grandmother's. Grandmother Lassiter probably hadn't wanted to take the master bedroom, either—the one her daughter had shared with Steve Douglas. The man Grandmother Lassiter believed was her daughter's killer.

Finally Macy settled on the small room at the back. A search through various closets revealed a stack of clean sheets. She made up the bed, trying not to think about actually sleeping here. The thick branches of the trees outside blocked most of the glow from the streetlight, throwing the room into deep shadows when the lights were out. The house was too large, too lonely and way too silent for her to feel comfortable.

She glanced inside the bathroom. Forget a shower tonight. No way was she brave enough for that. Macy paused in front of the dressing table, looking at her reflection. The face staring back at her wore a nervous expression. She swallowed hard, refusing to speculate on what she was afraid of—she knew, she just didn't want to face it.

She was afraid she would remember too much. More than she could handle. On this, her first night in the house.

The phone shrilled, shattering the silence.

Startled, Macy jerked as if she had been stung. Who could be calling at this hour? There was a phone in Grandmother Lassiter's room. She scurried down the hall, catching it on the fourth ring.

A harsh voice that she took to be male grated over the line. "Are you enjoying yourself in that house?"

She almost dropped the receiver. "What? Who is this?"

"You don't belong here. If you want to live, get out of there while you still can."

Click.

Macy stared in shock at the receiver. *If she wanted to live?* Who had been on the other end of that line? Someone who knew she was in the house. Someone who didn't want her there. Had news of her returning to Walnut Grove reached the ears of her mother's killer?

She turned her head to look at the window. Was the caller standing outside watching? Or was he in the house with her? If he was using a cell phone he could be anywhere. How could she turn out the light and behave as if nothing was wrong?

God, are You listening? I'm afraid. Please...watch over me. Help me make it through this night.

She sat rigid, straining to hear. Was she really alone? Or was someone lurking downstairs waiting until she fell asleep? She thought about calling the police but she wasn't sure she trusted them, and she didn't know Nick well enough to call him in the middle of the night.

Finally she went to bed, only to lie there staring at the ceiling, straining to hear. Something creaked. A footstep on the stairs? She listened, nerves raw. Nothing. Probably just the normal sounds of an old house, but how could she be sure? She stared at the door, imagining a shadow lurking, peering into the room, but there was no movement. She tried closing her eyes, hoping to relax, but nothing helped.

Macy threw back the covers and crawled out of bed. The silence was too heavy, too full of danger—real or imagined—for her to sleep. For the past hour she'd been lying with her eyes wide-open, ears straining to hear and nerves stressed to the max. Now she strode down the hall, looking for something to distract her, anything to take her mind off the phone call and the few things she'd learned today. The house felt empty, dead. She shivered. Would life ever fill these echoing rooms again?

She slowed her pace, creeping past the room that had belonged to her parents, afraid of waking any of those long-forgotten memories. Facing them in the light of day was hard enough without confronting them in the dark and lonely evening hours. She felt the same way about her childhood room and its air of familiarity.

That left the room her grandmother Lassiter had used. Macy entered her grandmother Lassiter's room feeling as if she was violating Opal's privacy. She turned on the bedside lamp. The dark blue drapes and carpet matched the deepest shade of the striped bedspread. A worn Bible lay on the bedside table.

So both of her grandmothers had been believers. She sat down on the bed and picked up the Bible, thumbing through the fragile pages. Several passages were underlined, with personal notes written in the margin. The ninth verse of Joshua, chapter one, caught her attention.

Macy read it aloud. "'Have I not commanded you? Be strong and courageous. Do not be terrified; do not be discouraged, for the Lord your God will be with you wherever you go.'"

She read it a second time, comforted by its simple promise. God must have led her to this verse, because it was exactly what she needed.

A church bulletin fell out of the back of the Bible. Walnut Grove Community Church. This must be where her grandmother had attended.

Tomorrow was Sunday. She'd start getting acquainted with the citizens of Walnut Grove by going to church. The people there would have known Opal Lassiter. Some of them must have been her friends. At least it was a place to start.

Macy sat on the bed, pondering her situation and begging God to help her. Finally she went back to her room, carrying the Bible. After placing the worn book on her bedside table, she crawled back into bed, pulling the blanket up around her shoulders.

She closed her eyes, feeling comforted—for now.

Nick drove past the Lassiter house, checking to see if everything looked all right.

The lights were off except for the one in the foyer and one upstairs that was probably the hall light. This was his third time to drive past here tonight. He hoped Macy was okay. It had to be strange for her staying in that house by herself. He was on duty tonight and he'd continue making a pass down this street occasionally.

Not that he expected anything to happen, but there had been attempts to break in before she arrived in town. It paid to be careful.

Sam's suspicion that Macy was bent on stirring up trouble had left him unsettled. There was also Macy's conviction that her father was innocent. What was that based on? Nick's thoughts turned again to Macy Douglas.

Maybe it was the rather dramatic way they had met last night, but something about her had gotten to him. It was more than the way she looked, with that fiery hair and gorgeous eyes. There was something deeper, something more personal drawing him to her.

Part of it had to be her determination to discover what really happened to her parents. This wasn't a shallow woman. She had an appealing depth and a passion. As his father would have said, Macy was the real deal. If he tried to help in this search, he'd be seeing a lot more of her. He could handle that.

He waved at two kids on bicycles he knew. About time they were getting home. He thought about stopping and asking what they were doing out at night like this, but decided against it. They had just another block to go and he'd keep an eye on them. As often as he drove through this neighborhood checking on attempted burglaries at the Lassiter house, he knew every child and most of the adults.

Nick drove past the police station and saw Sam headed for his car. The chief motioned for him to pull in. He parked next to Sam's car and waited for him to walk around to face him. Sam leaned his hands on the door. "You seen the Douglas woman today?"

"Yeah, I've seen her. She moved into Opal Lassiter's house. Guess she's planning to stay."

Sam puffed out a blast of air. "That's what I was afraid of."

What was Sam's problem with Macy Douglas? He hadn't been a policeman back when the Douglas case happened, so he couldn't have been involved. The way he'd been acting, though, seemed as if he had a personal grudge against Macy.

Surely Sam wasn't one of the people he needed to watch. He liked and respected the guy, but this attitude about Macy Douglas was making him uncomfortable.

He glanced at his watch. Another hour and he'd be off duty. Then he could rest a bit, eat breakfast and go to church. He wondered if Macy would be there. Not that it was any of his business, but he wished he'd invited her to attend his church.

Nick waited for Sam to walk away, but Sam just stood there eyeing him suspiciously. "You taking up with that woman?"

"What woman?" He knew exactly what Sam meant, but right now he didn't feel like cooperating.

Sam grunted. "That Douglas woman. You need to stay away from her. She's trouble from the get-go. I don't want you hanging around talking to her while on the clock. And that's an order."

Nick pursed his lips, feeling contrary. "I'd think you'd want someone watching her to see what she's going to do next."

"You sure that's what you've got on your mind? She's a good-looking woman and I'd hate to see you get involved with whatever trouble she plans to stir up."

Nick thought about telling him that Macy didn't remember her parents, didn't remember living in that house, but that was her story to tell. "All she wants is to learn the truth. I can't see any harm in that. The way I see it, knowing the truth is always better than believing a lie."

"You go right on meddling if that's what you're determined to do, but don't come running to me when you get in trouble. And if you help divide this town, you can forget about your job security. You got that?"

"I got it." Nick watched Sam stomp toward his car. Really ticked off. That wasn't good. Maybe he should back off, forget about it, but his conscience wouldn't let him. Even if the truth destroyed his memories of his father. He hoped it didn't come to that, but from the way Sam was acting, Nick had a gut feeling there might be a surprise headed his way.

FIVE

The next morning, Macy unearthed a box of breakfast burritos from the bottom of the freezer and settled for one of those, washing it down with freshly made coffee, and then got ready for church.

As she backed out of the driveway, she wondered if she'd see Nick. She straightened the car, irritated at the thought. Why would she care one way or another? After all, he was practically a stranger. Although, against her better judgment, she found herself thinking about him and depending on him much more than she should. She needed to back off where Nick Baldwin was concerned, not let him get in the way or distract her from her goal. Still she smiled, thinking it would be nice to see a familiar face.

Macy found the church, a medium-size white stucco building. A tall steeple pointed toward the lacy clouds drifting over a bright blue sky. Inside, the sun glowed through stained-glass windows depicting scenes from the Bible. Macy walked the center aisle and took a seat about halfway down.

Across the aisle from her an older woman with white hair and piercing hazel eyes smiled a welcome. Another woman, seated in front of Macy, whose face held enough wrinkles to belie the youthfulness of her bleached-blonde hair, turned and gave her a cold look before dismissing her with an audible sniff.

All right. Not everyone would welcome her. Had she really expected them to? After all, she wasn't here because she wanted to win friends and influence people. She was searching for information and she'd take what she could get, where she could find it, even if she had to fight for every morsel.

Which wasn't exactly the right attitude for attending church. Was she misusing a worship service for her own personal reasons? Maybe she needed to get her priorities straight.

As she stood to leave after the closing hymn, a warning tingle rippled up her spine. The hair on her arms prickled as she felt an almost visible wave of hostility wash over her. Stunned, Macy grasped the back of the seat in front of her so tightly her knuckles whitened. Her eyes searched the congregation. No one seemed to be paying attention to her, and after a moment the sensation of being watched—of being hated—eased. She took a deep breath and released the back of the wooden pew.

The blonde shoved past without a glance in her direction, but the older woman stopped to talk. "Macy? I'm Hilda Yates. I was a friend of your grandmother Lassiter."

Macy gripped her hand, grateful for any show of friendliness. "I'm so glad to meet you. I haven't been in town very long, and I'm just starting to get acquainted."

People milled around, heading for the door, but Hilda ignored them, and Macy tried to do the same. But she couldn't forget that someone had been staring at her earlier with a hatred so strong she actually sensed it.

"Opal loved you very much."

Loved her? Seventeen years with no contact from the grandmother who supposedly loved her so much? She wasn't that naive. "I'm sorry, but I never knew her."

Hilda's expression changed in some subtle way. "That wasn't your grandmother Lassiter's fault. She tried but your grandmother Douglas blocked all her efforts."

A rush of heat flooded Macy's face. She wouldn't listen to this criticism of the grandmother who had raised her, the only person who had ever been there for her. It was too much to expect. "That isn't true."

"I'm sorry, but it is. I saw her cry too many times when her letters and gifts came back unopened. However, this isn't the time or the place to discuss it." Hilda walked away, leaving Macy shaken and close to tears.

God, help me. I'm not sure I can do this. It's so hard.

How could she bear hurtful comments about her grandmother, the only family she had ever known? Was that what she could expect from the people here in Walnut Grove? If that was what they thought, they hadn't known the real Mattie Douglas.

Unwillingly, she remembered her grandmother's refusal to discuss the past, her belief that her son's in-laws had helped convict him, and a nagging, unwanted thought occurred to her. Was there a grain of truth in Hilda's accusation? She had to keep an open mind, listen to what was being said, no matter how much it hurt. She was beginning to realize this quest for the real story could change her in ways she hadn't expected.

And once changed, she knew she'd never be the same.

Nick waited outside the church for Macy. He'd seen her enter, but decided it might be better if he didn't approach her until after the morning service. She was stepping right along, cheeks flushed, looking as though she'd already tangled with someone. Her lips were set in a tight line and those eyes were flashing green fire.

He stepped in front of her, blocking the way. "Morning. Enjoy the service?"

"The service was fine."

She bit off the words as if they tasted bad, and Nick hoped she hadn't run into one of the more outspoken citizens who'd trashed her father. He'd like to shield her from that if he could, although he knew it would be impossible. Too many people had opinions of Steve Douglas, some good, some very bad. He hoped they wouldn't take it out on Macy.

He made an attempt to defuse the situation. "Look, you have to eat, and I doubt if Opal kept much on hand. How about going out to lunch, or if you'd rather we can get takeout and go back to the house?"

Macy looked as if she wanted to refuse, and he held up a hand, stopping her before she had a chance to say anything. "Probably the house would be better. We can talk about what's bothering you in private."

She stared at him for a moment, then heaved a sigh. "All right, I guess."

Good. That was a start. "Fried chicken okay?"

"It's fine."

"You go on home and I'll be there in a few minutes." He called in the order on his way to the car, and drove to the take-out place to pick it up.

By the time he got to the house she'd changed into jeans and a long-sleeved shirt the same shade of green as her eyes. Her burnished-copper hair tumbled in glossy waves to caress her shoulders, and her lips were curved in a welcoming smile that warmed his heart. This was one beautiful woman, and he couldn't deny the way she affected him. His mind was telling him to ignore how he felt, but his heart wasn't listening.

He carried the bags and cardboard boxes to the kitchen where she had arranged plates and silverware. Their hands touched as they set out the containers of coleslaw, potato salad and chicken. Although it was just a quick brushing of his fingers against hers, he felt a surprising warmth, a sense of awareness that was new to him.

Macy filled glasses with ice for the Pepsi he'd brought, and they sat down at the table. He said the blessing. She'd talked about God as if she were acquainted with Him, so Nick didn't suppose she would object to something that was an everyday part of his life.

They ate in silence for a few minutes and then he glanced at her over a fried chicken leg and figured it was time to talk. "What happened at church that bothered you so much?"

Her green eyes turned stormy. "I met Hilda Yates."

And that was why she was upset? Hilda was a nice person most of the time, if a little outspoken. So what had she said or done that had riled Macy? "Hilda was a close friend of Opal's."

"That's what she told me."

He waited while she took a drink of Pepsi before looking at him. "She said my grandmother Lassiter tried to stay in touch with me, but my grandmother Douglas blocked her calls and returned her letters unopened."

Okay, this wasn't what he had expected. He had assumed someone, Hilda maybe, had said something about her being in town and living in the house, or maybe mouthed off about her father. "So, what do you think?"

"I tried to deny her accusations, of course. But she just turned her back and walked out."

"How sure are you that it didn't happen?"

"I'm positive. My grandmother Douglas would never have done something like that, but I'm just beginning to realize how little I really know about what happened to my parents and how it damaged every member of my family."

He hadn't seen that before, but he was starting to understand how she felt. A violent crime didn't just destroy the victim; it ruined the lives of everyone who loved him or her.

He shoved his plate aside and leaned his arms on the table. "How did it go last night? Everything all right?"

She looked at him, and he knew something bad had happened. "Well, I had a phone call."

Nick took a drink of Pepsi, trying to act casual, even though he braced himself for what she had to say. "Who was it?"

"It was a man. He asked if I was enjoying myself, then he told me to get out while I could if I wanted to live."

Nick choked, sputtering Pepsi over the table. He grabbed a napkin to clean up the mess he'd made, stunned at what he'd heard. "He said *what*?"

She repeated the threat, looking lost, while Nick stared at her. What was going on here? Someone had threatened to kill her if she stayed in this house. So what was hidden here that someone wanted enough to pull something like this? Or did the person just want to get her out of town before she found out something better left secret?

He wanted to reach across the table and take her hand, tell her it would be all right, but she'd know he was lying. Nothing would be all right until they found the truth about Megan Douglas's death and learned for certain who had killed her. Most important, he had to find the jerk harassing Macy before the situation turned deadly.

"Is that all? Don't hold anything back. If I'm going to help you I have to know everything." He burned with the need to do something, anything, to make this threat go away. She had to talk to him, give him details, descriptions, anything that would help him.

She raised her eyebrows. "Everything?"

"Every threat, all of your fears, every bit of information that applies to this house and your parents. I need to know, and I'm depending on you to tell me."

She sat there staring at him, looking as if she might rebel. It wouldn't surprise him if she did, and that worried him. He was learning that Macy Douglas wasn't quick to rely on anyone. Somehow he had to convince her to trust him.

Her eyes were narrowed, her lips tight; this woman was as stubborn as she was beautiful. A fascinating combination, or it would be if he weren't so worried about that phone call. As a cop, he'd learned to take all threats seriously. Besides, right now he had too much to worry about to be concerned with anything personal. All right, he knew that wasn't true and it was one of his problems. From the moment he'd met her, his feelings toward Macy Douglas had been more personal than he liked or understood. Somehow he had to ignore the way just being with her affected him and focus on who was harassing her. Do his job as a police officer.

"Look Macy, I'm not trying to pry into your life, I

just want to help you. How can I do that if I don't know what's going on? Work with me on this, okay?"

After a long hesitation, she nodded, but he could tell she was reluctant to commit. If he was smart he'd mind his own business, walk away from this house and this woman and forget about it—forget about her. But for some reason, he couldn't leave. She needed him, and he was going to help her, regardless of how he felt about it, or whether she wanted him to or not. He was also going to learn the truth about what happened back then. Prove to everyone that his father had nothing to do with it. That was his main goal and he had to stick with it.

And it was time he got started. They talked for another half hour, until Macy seemed calmer, more relaxed. He felt easier about leaving her alone. When he left, his intent was to spend the rest of Sunday afternoon trying to learn more about Steve and Megan Douglas. The problem was that the case was so old, it would be difficult to know where to start. The town had been extremely divided back then and he had no idea who had been friends or enemies, so how would he know the truth when he heard it?

His thoughts turned to Macy. He hated to think of her alone in that house. The phone call could have just been harassment, someone resenting Steve Douglas's daughter coming to town. Or it could have been someone much more dangerous—a killer who didn't want to be discovered. He couldn't ignore that possibility. Someone had killed a woman in that house *and* hurt a child. He probably wouldn't hesitate to attack another person.

Macy had mentioned Hilda Yates. Maybe he'd stop by and talk to her. Hilda had been a close friend of Opal Lassiter. She might have some information he could use.

Soon he was seated in Hilda's living room. "Macy Douglas said she talked to you at church."

Hilda shot him a questioning look. "She did. We had a disagreement and I walked out. I told her the truth, but she didn't believe me, and I didn't feel like church was the place to get into an argument."

"So you're sure Opal tried to contact Macy?"

"Of course I'm sure. I saw some of her letters. They were unopened and stamped 'Return to Sender.' I saw Opal cry over them."

Nick thought about Macy and how positive she was that her grandmother Douglas wouldn't do a thing like that. She was bound to find out the truth and he knew it would tear her apart. He hated thinking about it. Hilda was looking at him as if trying to decide whether to say something. He waited, giving her time.

She nodded as if she had reached a decision. "Look, Nick, there's something I need to tell you. Along toward the end, Opal had acted strange. From some of the things she said, I got the impression she was changing her mind about a few things. Like maybe she was thinking someone other than Steve killed Megan."

Nick stared at her, dumbfounded. This really wasn't anything he wanted to hear. "Are you sure about that?" His voice came out harsher than he intended, but Hilda didn't seem to notice.

"Reasonably sure. Of course, I don't have any proof, but it's something to think about."

It was indeed, and he didn't like the implications. Not after the things Sam had said. So had Opal Lassiter believed the police sent an innocent man to prison? Then who did she think had killed her daughter? And what had changed her mind? He was just getting started in the investigation, and what Hilda said about Opal was one more piece of information to mull over. Yes, he knew it was an option, but it was one he didn't want to think about. He had a feeling he wouldn't be able to ignore it, though. This was the second time someone had mentioned the possibility that the police had messed up the investigation back then. The accusations probably wouldn't go away.

When Nick left Hilda's he decided to drive by and see Macy again. Not that he had a reason, he just wanted to check on her. Since he was off duty until tonight, it wasn't any of Sam's business what he did. At least he could pretend to believe that anyway, until he got caught. Sam had a temper, and he'd been clear that he wanted Nick to stay away from Macy Douglas. Which was harder to do than he had expected. Something about her kept calling him back.

And he didn't know how to deal with it.

did or did not do to you has nothing to do with me." Unless of course he was the one who had killed her mother.

His eyes bored into hers. "It has everything to do with you. I hear you're hoping to nail someone else for wiping out Megan. Well, you're wasting your time. Steve Douglas was a vicious piece of trash who wouldn't hesitate to destroy anyone who got in his way—including his own wife."

"The way he is supposed to have destroyed you?" The words slipped out before she could stop them, and as soon as they left her mouth, she knew she'd made a mistake. His face flushed so bright Macy wondered if he was going to have a heart attack right there in the grocery store, or if he would choke on what he was trying to say before he could get it out.

"Supposed? Supposed to have destroyed me? He ruined me, and for no reason other than he belonged to a different political party. He got just what he deserved, and from what I've heard, you're just like him. We don't need another Douglas in this town."

He whirled and strode away, leaving her staring after him. She wouldn't have believed the hatred he had for her father if she hadn't seen it with her own eyes. Could he have been involved in making sure Steve Douglas went to prison? But his words haunted her. *Anyone who got in his way, including his own wife?* What could her mother have done that would have caused a problem serious enough to get her killed?

When she got home from the store, Macy decided to skip evening worship service. No way was she coming back to this house after dark. She had at least one enemy in Walnut Grove: the man who had called her. And Sam Halston wasn't too thrilled with her being here. Neither were Raleigh Benson, her grandmother's attorney, or that blonde at church this morning. Add whoever had been staring at her at the end of the worship service and Garth Nixon, and the list was growing.

She didn't care how long the list was. Well, that wasn't true. Of course she cared. She was scared stiff about half of the time, but no matter how people felt about her being here, she had things to do, and she needed to get busy. Since she had a couple of hours before dark, she'd spend the time going through the house, trying to find something that might stir some hidden memory, no matter how elusive.

Macy started with her parents' bedroom, ready to tackle it in daylight, but a diligent search through the dresser and bedside tables revealed nothing. She stood for a moment, glancing around the room at the burgundy, blue and green floral queen-size bedspread and the walnut tables holding elegant lamps with crystal bases. A group of photographs was arranged on the chest of drawers, and she paused to look at them. One caught her attention, her father, her mother and her, the only photo of her father she had seen in this house. A picture flashed through her mind of the three of them in a park where there were swings and a slide.

They had been there the day of her mother's murder.

Macy strained to recall more, but the memory had faded. She slumped down on the bed, burning with frustration. These brief flashes, just enough to give her a glimpse into her past, were tearing her apart.

Blinking back tears, she got up and turned to check the closet, not really expecting much, but at least she could look. She slid open the doors and discovered clothing for both a man and a woman hanging there, as if waiting for the people who owned them to come back.

Macy wiped her eyes. For seventeen years those forlorn-looking garments had been hidden behind the sliding wooden doors. Clothing her father and mother had worn. Her heart burned. She would never see her parents again, and she didn't even have memories of them to comfort her.

She reached a trembling hand to remove a pale green dress of a soft, thin material from a padded hanger. Macy buried her face in its folds, and for a moment, the fragrance of lilacs seemed to hang in the air. She had a vivid memory of her mother wearing this dress, a memory of sunshine and laughter...and love.

Macy sank into a wicker rocker, holding the garment in her lap, struggling to remember more, but the memory was already dying. Finally, limp and dejected, she went downstairs, taking the dress with her. Halfway down she jerked to a stop.

The front door stood wide-open.

She had shut and locked that door, so how could it be open now, and who was here? Macy crept down the last few steps, trying to be as quiet as possible. The air crackled with tension. She paused on the bottom step, listening.

Silence.

But the house didn't feel empty—no sound, no movement, just a sense of not being alone. Macy tiptoed to the living room doorway and glanced inside, but no one was there. A search of the other downstairs rooms revealed nothing out of the ordinary and no intruder. So who had unlocked the door? And where was the person now?

She finished searching the rooms, ending in the foyer

again. A picture lay on the mahogany table. A picture of her father in prison clothes. Her eyes were drawn to a sheet of paper lying beside it and the words written there.

Steve Douglas got what he deserved. If you stay here, you'll deserve what you get, too.

Macy caught her breath, the hairs on the back of her neck prickling. That picture hadn't been there when she came downstairs. She would have seen it. She stood rigid, straining to hear something. The house felt empty now, but she couldn't be sure. She inched away from the picture, heart pounding. Still holding her mother's dress, she backed toward the front door. The person who had left that picture could still be hiding here, waiting to attack as soon as she turned to run. She needed to get out of this house. Get to someplace safe. Macy slid one foot behind her, moving slowly.

Quietly.

She bumped against something solid…and alive. Arms closed around her. A warm breath tickled her hair. A deep baritone voice said, "We've got to stop meeting like this."

The pressure in her chest eased. She twisted around, coming face-to-face with Nick. His arms still held her close to him and a mischievous grin curved his lips. Suddenly his expression changed, his eyes narrowing.

"What's wrong, Macy?"

"Someone was here." She managed to get the words out, past a throat gone dry and gritty, as if she had swallowed sand.

"Where? Inside the house?"

She nodded, and he gently moved her aside. "Stay here. I'll take a look."

Macy caught his arm. "I think whoever it was is gone, but he left me a present."

She indicated the picture and note, watching as he stepped toward the table. He didn't touch either one, just leaned closer, examining them. Finally he turned to face her. "When did you find them?"

"Just now. I was upstairs and when I came down the door was open. I looked through the rooms, but I didn't find anyone. When I came back through here I found the picture and saw the note. But it wasn't there when I came downstairs. I'd have seen it."

"So someone left it while you were checking out the rooms." He touched the garment she held. "What have you got there?"

Macy looked down at the crumpled fabric clutched tightly in her arms. "A dress. It's my mother's. I remembered her wearing it. That's all I remember, just that she wore it and I was with her."

He pursed his lips, looking thoughtful. "All right, let's back up. You came downstairs and the front door was open. I assume you didn't leave it ajar, is that right?"

Macy glanced at the door, feeling again the shock of finding it open. "No, I've been keeping it locked. I went upstairs to look around and when I came back it was standing open, but whoever opened it was hiding."

The implications sank in. Someone could come and go in this house as he pleased. She could have been attacked, killed the way her mother had been, and no one would have had any idea who had done it. So did her mother's killer have a key, and had he used it here? Had he used it that night? Or had he rung the doorbell and been invited in? She wondered where her father had been, and why he hadn't been home with his wife and daughter.

She had too many questions, and no answers. Nick was talking, and she had missed it. "What? I didn't catch that."

He stared at her. "Are you all right?"

"Of course I'm not all right. I have enough trouble staying here without someone being able to come and go without my knowledge. How would you like that?"

"I wouldn't." He pulled out his cell phone. "And we're going to do something about it right now. Let's get your locks changed and the alarm fixed. You can't stay here if someone can get in anytime they want to."

Macy zeroed in on what he had said. "Get the alarm fixed? I'd forgotten you said my grandmother Lassiter had an alarm but it wasn't working. What's wrong with it?"

He shrugged. "I don't know anything about alarms, don't have any idea how the things work, but the guy who was trying to break in back then did something to it. I'll get Joe out here and he'll make sure it's fixed and show you how to use it."

Macy considered this for about one second. "Get him here. I can't spend the night in this house the way it is now."

She had slept here thinking she was safe while someone could have unlocked the door and crept up the stairs to murder her in her bed. She shivered, suddenly chilled. That phone call. Could the person who had left the picture be the same one who had made the threatening call? What could have stopped him from sneaking up the stairs last night and killing her the way someone had killed her mother?

* * *

Nick made his call, and after he checked out the house to make sure it was clear he called the station and let them know what was going on. Then they waited in the kitchen for the locksmith to arrive.

Macy poured the last of the Pepsi, and they sat talking quietly, or Nick talked. Apparently Macy didn't feel up to holding a conversation just yet. She still looked vulnerable and he noticed the way her hands trembled.

Nick felt guilty. He hadn't meant to scare her like that, should have had more sense. He remembered the way his arms had closed around her, the way she had clung to him. Gradually she relaxed, growing calmer, as if she felt safer now that he was here. Or at least he liked to think she did. But he couldn't stay. Sooner or later he would leave and she'd be here, alone and vulnerable. Just thinking about it worried him all over again.

Macy hesitated for a minute, her expression suddenly uncertain, as if she wanted to say something but wasn't sure. He waited. "Nick, where was my father the night my mother was killed? If he wasn't here then he must have had an alibi for that time."

Nick shook his head. "Look, Macy. It happened a long time ago. I was just a kid, and by the time I grew up it was old news. That's one of the things we have to find out, but I haven't had a chance to go through the file yet. I hope to get to that tomorrow. I'm off work until tonight and then I'll be on patrol." And he didn't want Sam to catch him reading it. Not after he'd been warned to back off. No point in stirring up trouble between him and his boss until he had to.

She rubbed her forehead, as though she had a headache coming on. "There's so much I don't know, and I have no idea where to start. I'm not finding anything here. At least not so far."

"Don't give up. We're just starting to ask questions. We're bound to learn something."

"Is Sam still so opposed to me being here? I have to wonder what he's afraid of. My other grandmother believed the police had a hand in making sure my father was convicted. That they knew he was innocent, but they protected a guilty man."

Nick sat looking at her, trying to figure out how to deal with this. He'd heard the same thing from Sam, but everything within him denied the very concept. He couldn't accept it—refused to believe it. All his life he had tried to live up to what his father had been, always feeling he fell short. Macy was watching him, as if she wondered why he wasn't saying anything. The question in her eyes sent his mind reeling. Somehow he had to come up with something that sounded positive.

He shook his head, denying her accusation. It was one thing for him to be forced to think about it. It was something else to hear her say it out loud. Before he could openly admit it was a possibility, he'd need some very strong proof, and that proof wasn't out there. He'd stake his life on that.

"That's a serious charge. I'd go easy on saying things like that until you have more information. You need the police on your side, and this is no time to build walls between us. If you expect to learn the truth, you'll need our help."

She stared at him, and from the little he'd learned about her, he knew she'd be too stubborn to back down. He had to try, though. "Look, Macy, you've cut out a difficult enough job for yourself. Don't complicate it any more than you have to by taking on the police department. Wait until you know more about what you're facing, okay?"

He waited, hoping she'd agree. He wanted to do some digging on his own concerning the trial, and he didn't want her slowing him down. And he definitely didn't want her or anyone else even hinting his own father was involved. His dad had been a decent man, a good, staunch Christian. Angus Baldwin wouldn't have done anything that went against what he believed in and stood for.

Nick took a deep breath, staring down at the table, struck by sudden doubt. He quickly pushed the thought aside. He was right. He had to be.

Learning he was wrong would rip him apart.

Macy folded her mother's dress and placed it on the table. Nick watched, noticing her tense expression. Living here had to be hard on her. He couldn't do anything about that, but he'd make every effort to find out who was harassing her and put a stop to it. That was his job as a policeman. No, someone was doing more than harassing her. The person was threatening her, actually raising the possibility that her very life was at stake. He couldn't just walk away and forget that.

He also couldn't forget the way Macy had felt in his arms. Soft, sweet and as if she belonged there. Somehow he had to learn the truth about her mother's murder, not just focus on what he believed to be true, but make a concerted effort to learn the real role the police had played in the investigation. And he had to find a way to keep her safe. A tall order and one he couldn't accomplish without God's help.

Nick knew his own limits. Some things he might be

able to pull off, some he couldn't, but God didn't have limits. A phrase from last week's church sermon flickered through his mind. *I can do all things through Christ who strengthens me.* He had a feeling the time had come to put his faith to work.

A few minutes later a truck pulled into the driveway and locksmith Joe Tipton got out. Nick introduced him to Macy, wondering whether he'd be friendly or resentful because she was Steve Douglas's daughter. The town was so divided that it was impossible to anticipate anyone's behavior. But if Joe had reservations about Macy, or visiting the Douglas house, he probably would have come up with an excuse to stay away. Nick watched, ready to step in if necessary.

Joe wiped a hand on the seat of his pants and held it out. "Pleased to make your acquaintance, Macy. I was a friend of your dad's. He was a good man. Didn't deserve what happened to him."

Macy gripped his hand, smiling. "It's good to hear you say that. Not many people I've met in Walnut Grove speak of him that way."

Joe nodded his head. "You just pay them no never mind. Some people don't have a lick of sense where politics are concerned. Your mom and dad were good people and someone in this town knows more about what happened that night than they've bothered to tell. There was some dirty work going on, you can be sure on that."

Nick decided he'd talk to Joe later. Maybe he knew something that could help them. Or if not, he might know someone who did. At least it would be a place to start. He decided not to dwell on what Joe had implied— that something hadn't been on the level with Steve's arrest. That was another thing he'd ask when Macy wasn't around. Regardless of how he felt personally, he had to at least check into the possibility.

He didn't really have a choice. It was his job as a police officer and his duty as his father's son. *Do the best you can and do it right.* He'd heard his father say it too many times to ignore it now. That was the way he'd been brought up.

He'd never heard anything against the police in all his years of living here. Now the accusations seemed to be coming from all directions. Somehow he would get to the bottom of this, and he suspected when he found the truth it would confirm that Steve Douglas was guilty of murder. He'd do all he could to help Macy because he felt sorry for her, but he'd also do all he could to clear his father's name, too. That had to be his main focus.

Nick hovered over Joe, wanting to help, but not knowing where to start. He wasn't all that good at mechanical work. All he'd ever wanted was to be a policeman like his dad. Now it was all he really knew how to do. Maybe he should make an effort to learn to do practical stuff. It might come in handy someday. Right now he felt sort of useless, particularly in front of Macy Douglas. But since he didn't have a clue how to help, maybe he should just get out of the way and let Joe work.

It took a while to change the locks and install a new alarm, but Nick felt better when it was finished. Knowing the house was secure made him feel more comfortable about leaving Macy here alone. What had happened today had upset him more than he wanted to let on. If someone could get in a locked house in broad daylight, nothing could stop a person from getting in at night.

Something else occurred to him. They didn't know whether this was the burglar who had been trying to get in, or someone else. And how did whoever it was get hold of a key? Maybe more than one person was after Macy. This was getting complicated.

Joe was a good man who knew what he was doing. Nick didn't have any doubts about that. His work would hold up. No one would get in this house now without setting off the alarm and rousing the neighbors. At least they'd be alerted if someone got in, and then they would do what they could to secure the house. Maybe it was a good thing that someone had tipped his hand by entering and leaving the message today. It had given them a chance to make sure that couldn't happen again.

As soon as Joe was satisfied the house was protected, Macy paid him. He left and Nick handed Macy the keys to both the front and back doors. "Here you go. That should solve the problem."

Or one problem, anyway. They still had plenty of others to deal with. And when he left here he had to drop by the office and file a report.

Macy took the keys, closing her hand around them as if she held a special treasure, her expression showing the relief she felt.

"Thank you for all you've done. I feel so much better knowing I have new locks and a working alarm. I don't think I could have stayed here tonight without them."

Nick gazed at her, thinking a man could drown in the sea-green depths of her eyes. He'd like nothing better than to just stand here enjoying her company, but he was on duty tonight. "Are you going to be all right now? Don't force yourself to do something you're not comfortable with."

She nodded, the movement making the gleaming strands of her hair shimmer in the overhead light. "It took a while for me to calm down, but I'm fine now. Having you and Joe here helped a lot."

Him and Joe? That wasn't what he wanted to hear. Nick puffed out a sigh involuntarily. What had he expected? After all, she barely knew him. He spoke reluctantly, wishing he could stay with her longer, but he had to get to work before Sam called, checking on him. "I guess I need to go now."

Was that disappointment he caught in her eyes? His heart jumped at the thought. "Look, Macy. You keep your phone handy and if you need help, call. I'll be here as fast as I can. I'll also drive by occasionally to make sure everything's all right."

"I will, Nick, I promise. And it's good of you to do that. I really appreciate it."

Her smile dazzled him. He reached out hesitantly, brushing a stray curl off her forehead. It was just as soft and silky as he had expected it to be. A cold wave of reality washed over him—he had to leave before this situation reeled out of control. Getting involved personally with Macy was the last thing he should do. He backed up a couple of steps. "Okay, if there's nothing else, I'd better get to work. I'll check on you tomorrow."

Nick closed the door behind him and walked to his car, thinking about Macy. He hated leaving her alone like that, but it was time to go, and not just because he was on patrol. He needed time to sort out his feelings. He was torn over the necessity of helping Macy and still protecting his father's reputation. Would he have to choose between the two of them?

The way he felt was totally new to him. Macy had invaded his life in a way he hadn't expected. He'd been a cop for several years. Macy wasn't the first woman in distress he'd met. Nor the only beautiful one he'd seen, but there was something about her that muddled up his thinking.

If he was going to help her, he needed a clear head. For both of their sakes, he had to back off, concentrate on finding out who was trying to harm her. He had to learn more details about Megan Douglas's murder and what made the police so sure her husband had killed her...before Macy paid the price.

SEVEN

Two days later Macy poured herself a glass of tea and sat down at the kitchen table, staring at the items she'd found in her grandmother's bedroom closet. A medium-size box, a cardboard file and a photo album. She swallowed a gulp of tea and reached for the shallow box first, sending up a silent prayer that something in here would hold information she needed. Macy pulled the box into her lap and turned back the flaps.

Letters. The box was full of them.

All addressed to her.

Not one had been opened, but each had been stamped "Return to Sender." Macy's hand flew up to cover her mouth in disbelief. Her stomach clenched. Here was proof that Hilda had told the truth. Her grandmother Lassiter had tried to stay in touch, but grandmother Douglas had blocked the attempts. No matter how much she hated to believe the evidence, she couldn't deny what was in front of her.

Macy bowed her head, cradling the box in her arms. Hot tears splattered on the cardboard and the envelopes. The grandmother she had known and loved, the woman who raised her, had done this. A sob ripped from her throat. How could she have done something so cruel?

Macy had known this search for the truth might lead to information that could hurt her, but never had she imagined this searing pain of betrayal. Grandma Douglas had kept these letters a secret—kept Macy from her mother's family. In addition to the seven years she'd forgotten, an additional seventeen years of life with her other grandmother had been stolen by someone she trusted.

After getting her emotions under control, she reached for the box again. Her hand trembled as she used a paring knife to slit open an envelope. She hesitated for a moment, breathing deeply, before removing the contents and slowly unfolding the sheet of paper. The words struck her like a hammer blow.

My darling Macy,
I don't suppose you'll ever see this, just as you've never seen any of the other letters I've written, and Mattie has apparently blocked my calls in some way. But I can't give up trying to reach you.
    I just want to tell you that I love you and I miss you terribly. What happened wasn't your fault, but you have paid a high price for it.
    I pray that someday we'll meet again.
Your loving grandmother Opal.

Macy gently placed the letter on the table and leaned back in her chair. Moments passed until she could get herself under control enough to sit up and open her eyes. After a few more minutes ticked by she managed to read a couple more, finding they were similar to the first. Her grandmother Opal wanted to see her, and Grandma Mattie had stood in the way. She was just beginning to understand how deeply the current of grief and rage had rampaged through their lives, like an underground torrent, destroying everything in its way.

How could such an overwhelming anger and hatred so totally consume a person? But then again, Mattie Douglas's son had been arrested and sent to prison for a crime she was convinced he'd never committed. He'd died there and she never saw him again. Until the funeral.

She wouldn't have had the money or the transportation to go see him, and she had been obsessed with protecting Macy from knowing what had happened to her parents.

Macy could understand how her grandmother must have felt, even though she Macy resented what it had done to *her*. She got up and strode toward the window. Her grandmother Lassiter had lived in this house. Lived alone. She had written loving letters to her granddaughter, made an effort to stay in touch, hoping at least one letter would get through the blockade.

Her grandmother Douglas had loved her, too. She had grown up feeling that love. But both women were mothers. Each had lost a child in a terrible way. Her grandmother Douglas grieving over the son she had lost, bitterly convinced he was innocent. Her grandmother Lassiter's daughter had been brutally murdered.

Macy stared unseeingly out the window, knowing if the two of them had just turned their problems over to God, he would have taken the bitterness from them. Yes, they would still have had to deal with the devastation of their loss, but they wouldn't have had to go through it alone. Trusting in God could have eased their burdens and given them peace.

She saw Nick's patrol car pull into the drive and waited with a disturbing impatience for the doorbell to ring. She hadn't expected to see him this morning, but just the sight of him comforted her in some way. The bell rang, and she hurried to answer. Her heart leaped in a disconcerting manner at the sight of Nick standing in the doorway, the sun caressing his dark hair. His lips were curved in that enticing smile she was beginning to know. The well-fitting police uniform gave him an air of confidence, of having everything under control. Macy took a step back. Nick Baldwin was one extremely handsome man.

His eyes sharpened, staring into her own. "What's wrong?"

She tried to make her smile more natural, knowing she had probably failed miserably. "Nothing. Everything's fine."

He shook his head, his expression stern. "Don't give me that. I can tell by looking at you that everything is a long way from being fine. Now are you going to invite me in or do I have to stand out here on the porch?"

Macy realized she might as well give in. He wouldn't back off until she did. She stepped aside, letting him enter. "It's just that I've been exploring."

He stopped, staring down at her. "What did you find?"

"It's in the kitchen. I'll show you." She led the way, not really wanting to share the letters with anyone, not even with Nick, but knowing this was another piece of the puzzling mystery of her life.

She sat down at the table, motioning for him to do the

same. After a moment, she indicated the box. "I found this in my grandmother's closet. It's filled with letters she sent me, but I never received."

His eyes shone with compassion. "I'm sorry. That has to be tough."

Macy nodded, not wanting to admit the truth, but knowing she had no choice, no matter how much it hurt to say the words. "Yes, it's hard to accept, and evidently Hilda was right. I guess I owe her an apology. Apparently my grandmother Douglas returned the letters unopened. I never saw any of them."

The gentle understanding in his expression almost unnerved her. He reached for her hand, his touch tender and comforting. "Don't let it hurt you. She must have had a reason."

She couldn't keep the bitterness out of her voice. "I'm sure she did. At least, it must have seemed so to her. But she hurt my grandmother Lassiter, and she hurt me." In ways she hadn't even begun to comprehend yet.

"Do you want to read any more?" Nick indicated the box.

Macy sagged against her chair. "No. But I know I have to. There might be something useful in them."

The thought of reading any more of those pain-filled pleas for a reply almost tore her apart. She wished she had never come to Walnut Grove.

But then she wouldn't have met Nick.

The thought rippled through her like an electric shock. Was she getting too attached to Nick Baldwin? That hadn't been part of her plan.

Nick watched Macy, noticing the slightly flushed cheeks, the way she avoided looking at him. He knew she was very upset by her discovery. He released her hand, feeling a subtle loss of warmth. He glanced at the box again, realizing how difficult it must be for her to read the letters. She was right. They needed to go through them, just in case they held something that would assist in the investigation, but he could help with that.

He cleared his throat. "Would you consider letting me read them for you?"

She stared at him, as if not sure he was serious. "Why would you do that?"

He shrugged. "It's just an idea. I'd take care of them, and you'd get them back. I just thought it might be easier for you if I read them. If I find any information I'll share it with you."

As he'd told her before, he couldn't talk about evidence in a case, but the letters belonged to Macy. He'd be careful of what he shared, but if it was something he could tell her without jeopardizing the investigation, he would let her know. And yes, there was an investigation. Not an official one, of course, or at least not yet, but he was looking around on his own.

She just sat watching him, as if trying to decide if he could be trusted. He wanted to reassure her, but trust had to be earned. She didn't know him very well yet, but she would before this was over. He waited for her to make up her mind.

Eventually she nodded. "It hurts me to read them. Maybe I can handle it later, but not right now. I guess it would be all right if you'll make sure I get them back."

"You can depend on it. As soon as I go through the letters and make any notes I'll return them. I doubt if we find anything useful in them, but it's one of the things we have to check. Have you had any more problems I need to know about?"

"No. I hope the new locks will stop anyone from getting inside, and there haven't been any more phone calls. I still have a feeling that someone is just waiting for a chance to get at me, though."

Nick had a hunch she was right, and it worried him. This house was too big, too empty, but he knew it would be useless to try to get her to move out, and she wouldn't ask anyone to stay with her. But he had a feeling her being here alone was just trouble waiting to happen. The earlier attempts at breaking in, the phone call, the unlocked and open front door with the surprise photo, all pointed to someone playing a dangerous game, and there was no way he could prevent it.

Nick took a deep breath, trying to pull himself together. He needed to slow down, keep his wits about him. He had a killer to catch, and if he wasn't careful his feelings toward Macy Douglas could get in his way. She had no idea how she affected him, and he had to keep it that way. Had to focus on the goal—learning the truth about what had happened seventeen years ago and what was going on now were his first priorities. He would read the letters, but he didn't expect to learn much from them. Just a job that had to be done—one he could spare her. He could tell from her expression just how hard this had been.

Macy reached out to touch the box. "It seems like everywhere I turn I hit a wall. I've been searching this house, but since I don't know what I'm looking for, how can I know if I've found it? Does that make sense?"

Nick nodded. "It makes a lot of sense, and I know exactly what you mean. I'm dealing with the same thing. I hear so many conflicting accounts of what things were like back with the initial investigation and I don't know which one is true. I'm just stumbling around in the dark." First Sam and then Hilda and Joe and each one believing his or her opinion was right. And he had barely started. Investigations took time. Time he wasn't sure Macy had if someone really was after her.

He had a few more people in mind he needed to talk to, and he doubted it would be possible to keep his actions from Sam. Sooner or later, he was headed for a confrontation he wasn't looking forward to, but he was committed to the search for the truth. Regardless of the outcome, he believed he was doing the right thing. He was sure it was what his father would have done.

"Look, Macy, all this happened a long time ago. People may forget important details and some older people who might have relevant information may have died."

"Then how can we hope to learn what really happened? We don't have much going for us, do we? I'm beginning to think this is an impossible task."

The despair and frustration in her voice haunted him. He had to reassure her. "Don't you believe it. We have God on our side. He'll lead us through, Macy. Don't ever doubt it."

"I want to believe, and most of the time I do, but it's hard when I can't see that we're really accomplishing anything."

Nick leaned toward her, arms resting on the table, thinking of how to say this. "That's the way it is with God. He doesn't always answer with some big sign. Sometimes we don't see what He's done until we've weathered the storm, and then we look back and find He was there all the time. We just didn't realize it."

* * *

Macy stared at Nick. Where had that come from? She knew he was a Christian, she just hadn't realized how strong his beliefs were. She felt a renewed hope stir. He was right. They had to keep on with what they were doing and leave the results up to God. She needed to focus on that. And she would. Grandma Douglas had taken her to church, made sure she learned about God. Now that she was facing more than she could handle on her own, she'd make a stronger effort to trust in the one thing she had going for her. God, who loved and protected her.

Nick was talking and she pulled her attention back to him. He tapped the table with one forefinger. "Now here's what we're going to do. You go through this house one room at a time. Keep notes. Write down anything that looks the least bit out of place. I'll keep notes, too, and then we'll sit down and go over them together. With luck, we'll see something that can help."

Except he'd been open that he couldn't tell her everything. That still rankled, though she understood his reasoning. She grudgingly agreed. "All right. At least by keeping records we'll have a database of sorts that might keep us from going over and over the same ground."

Although she hated to admit it, Nick's suggestion made sense, but the silence of the house seemed to intensify, as if it waited for her, hushed, watching, hoping to catch her unaware. Fanciful, she knew, but that's the way it felt, as if the house itself were her enemy, daring her to learn its secrets. It was too big, too silent and too empty. Living here was getting to her. Maybe she should consider Nick's suggestion that she spend the nights at a motel.

Macy shook her head, hating what she had become. A wimp. That's what she was. Running away like a coward. She hadn't been raised that way. Grandma Douglas would have been against her coming to Walnut Grove and this house, but once here, she would have expected her granddaughter to stay the course. And that was exactly what she intended to do.

It might help if she got out more, got acquainted with other people, not just the ones at church. She could eat out once in a while, talk to people she met. Somehow she had to unlock her past one step at a time. First she would apologize to Hilda Yates, although just thinking about those letters cut her to the heart. But since Hilda was supposed to have been such a good friend of her grandmother Lassiter, maybe she had a few more little tidbits she could share.

"Macy?"

She glanced up to find Nick looking at her with a quizzical expression. "What?"

"I asked if you'd found anything else."

She shook her head. "Just the letters."

No need to mention the cardboard file and the photo album. She'd look at them later when she was alone. She was beginning to trust Nick, but there were too many unanswered questions—some about him. After all, she didn't know him very well yet. It might be a mistake to be too quick to trust.

After Nick left, Macy thought about doing some more searching, but a nagging feeling of guilt wouldn't let her rest. Finally she picked up the phone and called Hilda Yates. When Hilda answered she seemed a bit cool, and Macy had a hunch that was her fault.

"Look, Hilda, I want to apologize, but I'd prefer to

do it in person. If you'll tell me where you live I'll come there, or we could meet somewhere else if you'd rather. I need to talk to you, one on one."

"I'll come to you. That seems like a good place for us to talk."

Macy hesitated. Now that Hilda had agreed, she wasn't sure this was a good idea.

Meet here? In her parents' house? She'd prefer to see Hilda somewhere else that didn't have such a connection to the past. But she reluctantly agreed. "All right. When do you want to come?"

"How about now? I'm just a short distance away from Opal's house. I could be there in the next ten minutes or less if that works."

"That'll be fine. I'll be looking for you." Macy hung up the phone and wandered through the lower floor, seeing it in a new way.

Opal's home.

She'd been thinking of it as her parents' house. A place where she'd once lived, ignoring the fact that her grandmother Lassiter had lived here for the past seventeen years. Opal had to have left her imprint on it, maybe changed it, and possibly that was interfering with her recollection of how it used to be. She hadn't thought of that.

True to her word, Hilda Yates parked in the driveway less than ten minutes later. She walked toward the house and Macy opened the door to face her. "Thanks for coming, Hilda. Do you want to sit in the living room?"

"I suppose that will be all right. Anywhere that's good for you will work for me."

Macy led the way into the living room and took one of the gold brocade chairs. Hilda sat down in the other and looked around. "I can just see Opal here. She had a hard time adjusting at first because Megan's body had been found in this room. But eventually she conquered her emotions and I believe she actually felt closer to her daughter in this house than anywhere else, just because Megan had once lived here."

Macy swallowed the lump in her throat. "I'm having a hard time adjusting, too. It might help if I could remember something, but I've lost track of the years I lived here. They're gone as completely as if they had never happened."

Hilda stared at her. "Are you serious? I mean, yes, I can see you are, but you're saying you can't remember even living in this house?"

Macy shook her head, and Hilda continued. "What about your parents? You remember them, don't you?"

"I don't remember anything about them. My memory begins when I woke up in the hospital with Grandma Douglas sitting by my bedside. She never talked about my parents or anything to do with my past."

"Weren't you curious? It seems as if you would have been."

Macy thought about how to answer this without making her grandmother look bad. "You have to remember I was badly injured at the time of my mother's death. Her killer slammed me with the poker, I assume, since Nick says the police found it beside me and thought I'd been hit with the same weapon that killed my mother."

Hilda looked a little abashed, which encouraged Macy. "And then again, my grandmother was sure my mother's family and the police here in Walnut Grove had conspired against her son. I never saw a picture of my mother until I came here, and I don't see many pictures of my father posted in this house."

Hilda seemed to be thinking about this. Finally she said, "It looks like two bitter women refused to see anything except their own loss."

Macy nodded her agreement. "And apparently they used me as the pawn. I denied what you said in church, but now that I've seen the box I've had time to think about it, there's some truth in your comment."

"Well, I know she did try to write to you because I saw the box where she kept the returned letters. She showed me some of them and they were addressed to you, but had never been opened. I didn't read any of them."

Hilda glanced around the room, then looked back at Macy. "Like I told Nick, at the last Opal was behaving rather odd, and from some of the things she said, I have a feeling she was coming around to Mattie's way of thinking."

"You mean she believed someone else killed my mother?" And Nick had talked to Hilda? He hadn't mentioned that.

"I think she might have been reaching that conclusion, or at least thinking about it. Look, Macy, I was Opal's friend. I'd like to be your friend, too, if you'll have me as one."

Macy saw the sincere warmth in her eyes, her concerned expression, and found herself starting to trust this woman. "I need a friend, and I'd be happy to count you as one of mine."

Macy hesitated, not sure if she should go further, but then decided to take the plunge. "I met Garth Nixon in the grocery store. He was very hateful."

Hilda looked at her for a minute before speaking, as if trying to decide what to say. "Some people sided with Garth, believing that Steve cost him the election. I'm not sure myself. Some of us believed that Steve was right. Garth was involved in some rather shady deals I couldn't approve of. I wouldn't have been able to vote for him, and it had nothing to do with your dad's editorial page in the *Tribune*. I just never could trust the man."

Macy considered this. She'd never heard this side of the argument before, and she'd assumed that most of the town supported Garth. "Did others feel that way? I've just been told how my father's editorials stirred up trouble and cost Mr. Nixon the election."

"Well, that's the original story, but about half of the town had a different opinion. Garth lost, that's true, but I don't know how big a part those editorials played in it, and how much it was caused by the distrust of the people who actually knew him."

Hilda glanced around the room again. "Look, Macy. This is a big old house and I realize you might not be all that comfortable staying here by yourself. Would you like for me to spend a few nights with you until you feel more at home?"

Macy smiled, appreciating the offer, but knowing she had to refuse. "That's sweet of you, but I'm hoping I'll start to remember something about my life here, and I have recalled a few small bits, but nothing that really helps. I have a feeling the memories may come back easier if I'm alone."

"I understand, but if you need me, I'm just a phone call way. I would do all I could to help you for Opal's sake, but now that I've met you, I'll do it for you, too."

Macy's heart warmed. She had made two good

friends in this town, Nick and Hilda. God was blessing her. She remembered how Nick had been protecting her since she got here. She found herself thinking about him when she should be concentrating on what she was here for. She needed to put everything else aside and focus on the goal she'd set for herself.

No man, even one as good-looking as Nick Baldwin, could be allowed to get in her way.

EIGHT

Macy glanced around the living room and decided she needed to get out and meet people. She wasn't going to get to the bottom of things if she just stayed cooped up here in the house. The people of Walnut Grove had known her parents, and someone out there had information she needed. It was time she started hunting for it.

She changed into fresh jeans and a light green T-shirt, thinking it was almost the same shade as her mother's dress. Another thing they had in common? Ten minutes later she walked into the Iron Kettle, a restaurant on the town square, and sat down. A couple of women sat in a booth by the window, one of them the blonde from church. The one who had snubbed her. She'd never seen the other one before.

Four men sat at a table, talking and laughing. An older man seated in a booth alone was reading a newspaper. So far, no one had seemed to notice her. Macy ordered a cup of coffee and sat back to wait, feeling like a piece of bait on a hook. Would anyone be interested?

After a few moments she became aware of furtive glances being sent her way from the older man, peering at her over the top of his paper. So far, no one else had seemed to notice her. The waitress brought her coffee and when she left, he got up and sauntered her way.

"You Steve's girl?"

She nodded, and he slid into the booth across from her. "You mind if I join you?"

Since he was already there, it would have been pointless to refuse. "Please do. I'm Macy Douglas."

He held out his hand. "Quent Harper. I knew Steve."

"And did you like him, or hate him?" She might as well get his feelings out in the open. So far the people she'd met fell into one category or the other. There didn't seem to be a middle ground.

Quent squinted at her for a second and then grinned. "Seems like you've run into some of the town's hardheads. Steve was all right. But a lot of people just don't have any sense when it comes to politics. He told it like it was, and it riled some of them."

Macy sipped her coffee. "So which side were you on?"

"Well, me and Steve saw things pretty much alike. Garth Nixon would have been a disaster. Crooked as a dog's hind leg, but he had a following. Still does, I guess, although he's pretty much washed up where politics are concerned."

Macy considered this, thinking of what to ask next. "I guess you know why I'm in Walnut Grove."

He folded the paper and placed it on the table. "Heard you were looking for a killer. You ever think you might get in serious trouble stirring things up like that?"

Think it? She'd had it drilled into her from practically everyone she'd met. Yes, she had a feeling that was exactly what she was in the process of doing, and she didn't have any idea which direction it would come from.

"I've thought of it, and you're probably right, but I have to do this. Do you have any idea who might have killed my mother?" Because everyone seemed to be overlooking that important question. It was as if her father's politics overshadowed everything else. As if the death of Megan Douglas wasn't all that important.

Quent seemed to know what she was thinking. "Makes us seem kind of self-centered, doesn't it? I'll bet most of what you've heard since you came here is about Steve. Not much about Megan. That right?"

Macy nodded. That was exactly the way it had been, and she needed to know why. Her mother had been murdered, and it was as if no one cared very much, except for her grandmother Lassiter. She was surprised at how much that hurt. Megan Douglas had been a victim. And she believed her father had been, too, and both of her grandmothers—and herself, for that matter. Someone had deliberately destroyed her family.

Quent tapped the tabletop with one forefinger. "Well, in a way, I guess it was like that. Sometimes it seemed like people were more interested in making Steve pay than they were in finding out what really happened."

Macy stared at him, wondering what his reaction would be to her next words. "My grandmother Douglas thought the police might be involved in making sure my father was convicted. Like they had a reason to want him to be guilty."

Quent shifted in his seat, as if uneasy. "I wouldn't be talking out loud about that if I was you. Feelings ran high back then, and there are some things you'd be better off not getting into. That just might be one of them."

Macy's eyes widened at the seriousness of his voice. The man wasn't kidding; he really believed what he was saying, so had her grandmother been right? And if so, what did it have to do with the present police? Or did Quent mean something else entirely, something she was missing?

A presence made itself felt. Someone hovered over them, someone who wasn't giving off friendly vibes. Macy glanced up to see the blonde standing there staring down at her.

Quent glanced up too, looking startled. "Anita—I didn't see you."

"No, apparently not." She shifted her attention to Macy. "I'm Anita Miles. I saw you at church."

And didn't seem all that happy about it. In fact, she didn't appear to be very enthused now, either. "Yes, I saw you, too."

"You're wasting your time trying to dig up dirt on anyone around here. Justice was served years ago when Steve Douglas went to prison. He got just what he deserved."

How dare this woman talk like that in a public place? It was almost like a personal attack. In fact, now that she thought about it, that was exactly what it was. "I don't think so, and I'm going to find out the truth."

Anita flushed. "You just might find out more than you want to know. Steve Douglas wasn't the shining knight on a white horse that you might be thinking he was. He was only human, and nothing special, if you want the truth."

Macy fought for control. "We all have our faults, things we want to hide. I wonder, what's hidden in your past?"

Anita leaned over the table, looking almost threatening. "Keep on the way you're going and you just might find out. And you could be biting off more than you can handle."

She whirled and strode toward the door where the other woman waited. Macy glanced at the group of men, noticing the self-conscious way they were glancing at one another, as if they were trying to pretend they hadn't noticed anything.

She looked back at Quent. "What was that all about?"

He shrugged, and she gave him a stern look. "No, you don't. I don't know that woman, never heard of her before, but she knew my parents. I need to know who she is and what her connection was with them. If you won't tell me, I'll find out somewhere else."

Quent sighed. "I knew I never should have sat down here. All right. That was Anita Miles. She used to be Anita Simms when she was younger. Talk was that she had her eye on Steve, but he married Megan. I guess she wasn't willing to leave it alone. Kept trying to get him interested in her. I never heard that he paid any attention to her, and maybe that's the reason she hated him so. She was one of the witnesses at the trial. Claimed he was having an affair with her."

Macy stared at him, feeling as if the breath had been knocked out of her. "Was he?"

Quent shook his head. "I don't think so. But Anita is a hater. You don't want to get on her bad side. Thinks she's something special. She also said he wanted a divorce but Megan wouldn't give him one. That he was talking about finding a way to get rid of her."

"Do you think she was telling the truth?"

She couldn't bear to think it. Nothing she had heard or believed had prepared her for this. Her father loved her. Her grandmother had said so. Hadn't he also loved the mother of his daughter?

Quent sat silent for a minute. "Well, she was a good-looking woman back then, and she kept throwing herself at him. I don't know what the truth is. My gut feeling says no, but I don't have one lick of proof one way or the other."

He got out of the booth. "I'm glad to have met you, Macy. But I think you may be taking on more than you can handle. You might ought to leave Walnut Grove. Nothing you can do now can help either Steve or Megan. But it *can* get you killed."

Nick was driving by and saw Macy leaving the Iron Kettle and get in her car. He followed her on a whim, pulling in behind her when she parked in the driveway back at her house.

She stepped out of her car and turned to face him. He felt like someone had punched him in the stomach. She looked wiped out, stunned, like she'd walked headfirst into a brick wall. Oh, not in appearance—she looked great, the way she always did—but something must have happened to upset her like this.

He hurried to meet her. "Hey, you doing all right?"

She stared up at him, and he could see the confusion and hurt in her expression. Probably she'd collided with someone who had trash-talked her dad. From the way she looked, it must have been rough. "Macy? What's wrong?"

"Nothing."

He took her by the arm and led her toward the house. "You're not very good at hiding your feelings, you know that? Now something is definitely wrong, and I'm not leaving here until I find out what. So let's go inside and sit down and talk about it."

She pulled away. "What makes you think it's any of your business?"

"Well, there's the little matter of me trying to keep you alive, and the fact that I'm a cop trying to find out what happened with your family. Is that enough, or do you need more?"

There was also the problem of her getting under his skin, although he didn't want to talk about that. Every time he got close to her it was like there was something pulling them together. Something he didn't understand, but couldn't ignore. And that desperate expression on her face didn't help any.

She looked at him for a moment, then nodded and started walking toward the house. He followed, even though she hadn't exactly invited him. No way could he leave her now. He needed to find what was wrong and see if he could do anything about it. Nick refused to examine why he felt it was his responsibility. He just knew it was.

They walked in silence, with him striding along beside her, waiting until she unlocked the door and then following her inside. At least she didn't tell him to leave, which he felt was encouraging. Maybe she didn't really didn't mind his being here. "Where do you want to sit, here or in the kitchen?"

"The kitchen, I guess. And I suppose I should talk to you."

But she didn't want to. He could hear it in her voice. Better go slowly and give her time to pull herself together. And he preferred the kitchen himself. It seemed more intimate sitting across the table from each other.

Apparently she felt the same way, which made him feel good, but he wondered what had happened now. He sat down and watched as she moved around the room fidgeting with one thing after another. From what he could see, she was trying to postpone talking for as long as possible. That was okay. He was here and he wasn't leaving until she told him what was wrong. He could wait, no matter how long it took.

After a few minutes of killing time, she fixed two glasses of iced tea and sat down at the table.

"I was in the Iron Kettle and I met Quent Harper. He came over and introduced himself. He said he knew my father."

Nick nodded. He knew Quent. He was a pretty good guy. Set in his ways, but then most people were, including him, he guessed. "He upset you?"

"No, that was Anita Miles."

"Ah-huh." He knew Anita, too. Most people in town did. She wasn't one of his favorites, a pain in the neck most of the time. "What did she want?"

Macy rubbed her forehead. "I saw her in church, and she was unfriendly. Today she was...*hateful,* I guess is the only word for it."

"She's not exactly a ray of sunshine anytime. What got her back up today?"

"She more or less said my father was guilty and that I was taking on more than I could handle."

Nick leaned forward, taking her hand in his, feeling that warm shock of awareness he received every time he touched her. "Look, Macy. You knew you were going to run into this kind of thing. Don't let it bother you."

She glanced at him, her eyes full of misery. "That's not all. I made Quent tell me about her and he said she was one of the witnesses against my father at the trial. She claimed he was having an affair with her and that he wanted a divorce but my mother wouldn't give him one. She said he was talking about ways to get rid of his wife."

Nick realized he needed to talk to Quent. The files he'd read so far hadn't mentioned that Steve Douglas had been a womanizer. He wished with all his heart he could do or say something to help her, something to wipe the pain out of her eyes.

He'd questioned a couple of Steve's friends who had been sure he was innocent, and Garth Nixon's former campaign manager who claimed Steve was lower than dirt. That he'd ruined a good man by the lies he'd told about Garth. Although considering what Nick knew about Garth, he didn't have as good a view of the guy.

"Don't let it get to you, Macy. Anita isn't known for being all that truthful, and this happened a long time ago. We've got a lot to sort through before we learn the truth. Keep praying, keep trusting God and don't give up. You're not alone. We're in this together."

Nick realized how strongly he meant that. Macy Douglas had moved into his heart in a way he hadn't expected and had tried to fight against it. Now he'd do everything he could to bring her peace. Even if the truth convicted his father of doing wrong. Nick took a deep breath, praying it wouldn't come to that, but it was something he had to consider, no matter how often he tried to deny the very suggestion, or how much he hated even thinking about it.

Still, he couldn't go against the way he had been raised. He believed his father had lived his Christian beliefs, and he had to do the same. To do otherwise would not only be a betrayal of those beliefs, it would also be a betrayal of his father. He had to do what he thought was right. That was the way his father had lived. He hadn't seen proof of anything different so far, and until he did, he wouldn't stop believing in the man who had raised him. But he would also make every effort to discover the truth, no matter what it would be. He owed that to Macy.

The hope in her eyes went through him like a knife. Yes, he'd do all he could to learn the truth, but what if that truth hurt one—or both—of them? Would the relationship blooming between them be strong enough to survive?

Nick watched Macy, seeing the warring expressions fleeting across her face. She would seem receptive to what he was saying, and then in the next instant withdraw from him, looking wary. He sensed that she didn't fully trust him, which bothered him more than he wanted to admit. He had a feeling that trusting wasn't easy for Macy. He needed to back off, give her room. No, he didn't like it, but he had no choice. For now he would just have to do the best he could to earn her trust and leave the rest up to God.

"Listen to me, Macy. No matter where we go with this we're likely to run into people who say things that we won't like, even things that might hurt. If that happens, we'll just have to ignore it and move on. What you've set out to do is more important than someone's opinion of you or your parents."

She stared at him for a minute before slowly nodding her head. "You're right, of course. It's just that I want so much to believe they were both victims. That someone else killed my mother and then framed my father for the crime. I've lost so much it's hard to listen when some-one says hateful things about either one."

"I know. And I'll protect you from that as much as I can, but I can't always be there."

She sighed. "I understand what you're saying, but it's still hard. I guess I'll just have to toughen up and take it. After all, what I owe my family is more important than what anyone has to say. You don't have to worry. I won't fall apart again."

What she owed? She saw this as a moral task, just the way he felt about his father. He only hoped he could work his way through this tangle of lies and truths with-out destroying either one of them. But he was a cop. He had taken an oath. No matter what this turned up, even if what he discovered broke his heart, he would have to carry through. If he made it through this mess in one piece, he was going to need God's help—big-time.

Macy watched him. Would he really be there for her? He'd said it, but could she trust him? Did he really mean it? She'd been hurt before by trusting the wrong man. She was wiser now. Wise enough to know that a promise wasn't always worth the breath it took to make it. Some-thing about Nick said he might be different, though.

She'd already relied on him more than she wanted to, but he was always there. She thought about that. Always there? Yes, that described him. So maybe she could de-pend on him, after all. At least she hoped so, but there was a limit to what she could expect from him.

He leaned toward her…close…too close. She knew she should draw back, but instead she held her breath, waiting. Nick placed both hands on her shoulders, and she resisted the urge to lean toward him. His eyes stared into hers—direct, piercing.

"I meant what I said, Macy. I'm in this with you. Don't you ever doubt it. I'll do everything I can to help you, whatever the cost."

Whatever the cost? What did he mean by that? Was he putting himself at risk by investigating her mother's death? More important, was he hiding something from her? Could she trust him, after all?

He seemed to know what she was thinking because he released her shoulders and leaned back. Macy felt a sense of loss, as if she had thrown away something very precious. Done something she would regret later when she had time to think about it.

Nick's attitude became more businesslike, more of an officer than a friend. "Now, the first thing we have to discover is the name of the person who threatened you over the phone. I'm going over the police files, asking questions, but I'll need your help. You might talk to Raleigh Benson again and see what he can tell you about your parents and your grandmother."

Macy accepted the change in his attitude, hoping she hadn't offended him. She needed him too much to do that. Needed him? Was that the only reason she wanted him around? Feeling ashamed at the thought, she hastened to cooperate. "All right, I can do that. Anything else?"

"Not that I can think of right now. I'm going to see Joe Tipton and ask him what he knows. When he was here fixing the alarm he seemed to feel like your dad got a raw deal. Maybe he has some inside information that will help us."

Macy stared at him, feeling a glimmer of hope.

Maybe Nick really was serious about helping her. Could she actually have met someone she could depend on after years of having no one except her grandmother? She'd always felt left out when her friends talked about their families, about doing things with them, sharing with them. Her grandmother had always been there for her, but she had missed having a mother and father, sisters, a brother, all the things her friends had and she didn't.

There had been something dark hiding in Grandma Douglas, a certain sadness, preventing her from enjoying life. Macy understood that sadness now, but it had been disturbing when she was growing up. She remembered the way her grandmother would sit, silent, staring out the window, the way she occasionally brushed away a tear. A part of her wished she had known back then what was wrong. Perhaps she could have helped. But deep down, she knew nothing she could have done would have lightened the load. Only God could ease the burden of a mother grieving for her child.

She pulled her attention back to Nick, seeing the sincerity in his expression. "I don't know many people in town, and the ones I have met don't seem to want to talk to me, but maybe they'll be more open with you."

At least she hoped so. But with Nick helping her, she felt as though they had at least made a start on learning the truth about her past.

NINE

Macy opened the file she'd found in her grandmother's closet and spread a pile of newspaper clippings out on the table. The headline of the closest one confirmed her suspicion as to what they would be. Woman Murdered at 879 Oak Drive.

Her grandmother Douglas had a few newspaper articles, but mostly about the trial. Macy had searched the internet, but found only a couple of articles, one of which she already had read. After all, it had been seventeen years. No one cared that much anymore. No one except her. She found one she'd never seen and had a feeling it would be different. Macy stared at the yellowed clipping for a moment, trying to work up the courage to read it. Finally she lifted the article off the table and took a deep, steadying breath.

Megan Douglas, wife of prominent newspaper owner Steven Douglas, was murdered in her home last night.

Icy fingers wrapped around Macy's heart. There it was. In black-and-white. Had it been published in her father's newspaper? Probably. Since it was the only one in town as far as she knew. Had he written the article, stating the facts?

No. He couldn't have. Not if he had really loved her.

She read further, cringing at the description of the wounds on her mother's poor, battered body. How could any sane person kill a helpless, unarmed victim like this? Hurting her almost beyond recognition.

She'd never dreamed it would be this bad. Her mother, not just killed, but viciously attacked. She leaned back, eyes closed, struggling against the images the words brought to life. Not a memory, nothing like that, just word pictures painted by the author of the article. Pictures her unruly mind insisted on visualizing.

A shadowy wisp of something as fragile and tenuous as a drift of fog floated through her consciousness. A voice, harsh with anger. No, a much stronger emotion than anger. A voice hardened with hatred.

A voice strangely familiar.

You brat. Get away from me.

Macy tried to hold the memory, trying to remember who had said the words, but as quickly as it had come, the faint echo faded from her mind. She slapped the table in frustration. She wanted more. More than these isolated bits of memory that didn't seem to connect to anything. Would she ever know the truth? She pushed the clippings away, unable to continue reading.

Surrendering to an overwhelming desire to recall what she had thought she'd remembered, Macy leaned forward, hands over her eyes, struggling to call back the words, the memory of the voice, but the moment was gone. Finally she closed the file, feeling like an impostor. She might own this house, but would she ever truly feel at home here? Or would the horrible past that had stalked these rooms destroy her, too?

There was something she needed to do. Something

she had pushed aside for too long. It was time to act. Macy reached for the phone and called Nick.

He answered on the second ring. "What's wrong, Macy?"

"Nothing's wrong. I just want to visit my mother's grave. Can you give me directions to the cemetery?"

"I can do better than that. There's not much traffic out there and it might be better if you don't go alone. I'll be glad to take you. When do you want to go?"

Macy took a deep breath. This was too personal to share with anyone, but then again, maybe Nick was right. The cemetery might be isolated, no place for her to be by herself right now. Not with an unknown enemy out there just waiting for a chance to get at her.

She bit back her protests, grateful he was willing to take time to go with her. If she had to make this trip with someone, she'd rather have Nick than anyone she could think of. "Any time you're free."

"I'm not on duty until tonight. We can go now if you want."

Macy hesitated. Yes, she needed to see the graves, but was she ready for this? She forced herself to swallow her uncertainty. What was wrong with her, wavering back and forth all the time? Couldn't she just make a decision and stick with it? What had happened to the woman who always had to be in control? Evidently she had disappeared, replaced with a muddle-minded woman who didn't know from one minute to the next what she needed to do. No matter how seeing the graves affected her, with Nick beside her she could handle it.

"Now would be fine if you can get away."

"No problem. I'll be there in a few minutes." He ended the call, and Macy checked her makeup, locked the door behind her and waited for him on the porch. As soon as she saw him coming, driving a dark blue pickup instead of his police car, she got up and walked down to meet him. Nick leaned over, opening the door for her. His smile immediately brightened her mood. Being with him always made her feel better. She climbed in and looked over at him.

"Thanks for doing this. I appreciate it."

"Hey, I'm glad to do it. In fact, I should have suggested it before now. It's just a couple of miles from here."

"I guess I should have gone earlier, but everything else seemed to get in the way."

"Well, it's a nice day for a drive, and we'll probably be the only ones there."

Macy stared out the window as he drove away from town, wanting to talk, but so full of conflicting emotions she couldn't think of anything to say. She dreaded this trip, had kept putting it off, knowing that viewing the graves would be hard. If she could just remember her mother and grandmother, remember what they were like, it would be so much easier, but she felt so conflicted. A part of her wanted to grieve for them, but they seemed like strangers. People she'd heard about but had never met.

A sign pointed uphill in a wooded area on the outskirts of town. The road was just a dirt track, and a bit rough, but it opened out to a snug little cemetery on the top of a hill. Trees surrounded the clearing, and birdsong filled the air. Macy got out of the car and hesitated.

Nick took her arm and led her toward a row of tombstones. They walked slowly, with Macy stopping to read names and examine the brightly colored artificial floral arrangements, aware she was only putting off the moment when she would stand beside the graves of the two women who had been such an important part of her life. Women she couldn't remember and had no idea what they were like as real people. That seemed like an insult to them. She stumbled and Nick pulled her erect, drawing her against him. Macy took a deep breath, wanting to turn and walk away. Why was this so hard? It was just a couple of graves in a remote country cemetery. Why did she have this feeling of guilt as if she had betrayed them in some way?

Her father wouldn't be here. He was buried in Tulsa. Grandma Douglas was buried beside him. Something Macy hadn't realized until she had to make arrangements for her grandmother's funeral. Another secret that had been kept from her. She'd never been to the cemetery there, had no reason to go. Not until after her grandmother had died had she known her father's body lay in the adjoining grave site. That had been a devastating surprise on a day she'd had enough to deal with. Even thinking about it brought back the overwhelming sense of surprise and hurt she had felt on reading his tombstone.

Macy shook her head in amazement. Each mother buried by her own child.

A bitter, despairing sensation of being alone, of having no one, surged through her. Being here in this secluded plot of ground set aside for the dead brought home with a desperate finality just how empty and desolate her life really was. Her family was gone. All she had left was this driving obsession to see the monster who had destroyed them brought to justice.

Nick stopped beside the graves and Macy forced her

thoughts back to the present, reading the names engraved on the two tombstones. Opal Lassiter and Megan Douglas. She knew how her mother's life had been taken from her, knew in sickening detail, but she needed to find out how her grandmother Lassiter died. Had she been ill? Or was she a victim, too?

She paused, struck by the thought, wondering where that had come from, then dismissed it. If there had been anything strange about her grandmother's death, someone surely would have mentioned it. And right now was a good time to remember that she wanted the truth, not to spend valuable time wandering down emotional and mental side roads. She had to stick to the facts as she knew them.

Macy glanced around at the well-kept graveyard. An eagle perched on the branch of a dead tree off to the side, its snowy head and tail stark against the blue sky, but other than that the two of them were alone. She moved away from Nick, needing space. Her mother. Her grandmother. An overwhelming sense of loss assaulted Macy. Her knees buckled, causing her to slump between the graves, an outstretched hand resting on each mound of earth as she gasped out a prayer.

"God help me. Please. I feel like I've let them down by not being able to remember them. If You will…give me a memory of them and the love we shared. I need them…need to know them in my mind the way I once knew and loved them in my heart…please…"

Macy knelt there for a few minutes longer, aware that Nick waited, watching over her. She was glad he'd come with her. This was too hard, too devastating to face alone. She was beginning to realize that searching for the truth might not be what she had expected when she came to Walnut Grove. But she had a job to do, not only for her mother and father, but for both of the women who had raised and loved them. Tears cascaded down her cheeks as she got to her feet, more determined than ever not to let them down. With God's help she would never give up searching for the truth, no matter how long it took or where it led.

Nick stood silent, watching Macy. He could almost feel her grief, her emotion, touching him as if the two of them were connected to each other in some way. She knelt between the two graves, and he sensed she was praying. He sent up a prayer of his own, asking God to comfort her. This had to be hard. Suddenly he realized how alone she was, how vulnerable. She'd never mentioned other family members, friends, anyone who would be there for her. Was that why he felt the need to help her as much as he could? Did God have a reason for putting him in Macy's life? If so, he prayed he wouldn't let either of them down.

Although he wanted to reach out to her, he wouldn't intrude on her space. She needed to be alone right now. Alone with her family's graves. This was a tough time for Macy, but Nick believed God would calm her, give her the peace she needed so desperately. Still, he was grateful he could be there for her. She might need him later.

His own parents were buried here, but he knew how they had died, had lived through their funerals. Although it had been painful for him, he realized Macy was dealing with a more crushing problem. She couldn't remember her family members. He had good memories; she had nothing. He couldn't take the place of what she had lost, but he promised God that he would be there for her, and if it was at all possible, he would keep her safe and do everything he could to help her regain her memory.

Macy turned around to find Nick standing close behind her. He reached out and she stumbled into his arms. He held her in a gentle embrace. For a moment she leaned against him, as if drawing strength from his presence. His lips brushed her forehead as he murmured words of comfort. After a moment she stepped away, swiping at her eyes. "I'm sorry. I sort of lost myself for a minute."

He drew her back to him. "It's all right. I'm glad I could be here with you."

She leaned against him and he realized how much she needed someone; maybe she didn't actually need *him*, although he'd like to think so, but she needed someone to be here so she wouldn't be by herself. Visiting these graves alone would have been overwhelming. After a few minutes they walked back to the pickup.

Once inside Nick turned to look at her. "You all right?"

"I am now." Macy placed her hand on his arm. "Nick, thank you."

He gently stroked her cheek. "Anytime, Macy. You need me, I'll be there—whatever happens, whatever you need." He knew all too well he couldn't be there every minute, but he'd do everything humanly possible to keep her safe.

He started the motor and drove her back home. They didn't talk much, and he suspected she was thinking about the graves and the time they had spent there. When they reached the house he walked her to the door and hugged her again before he left.

She gazed up at him, her smile tremulous. "Thank you for going with me. I can't express how much it meant to me."

"I'm glad you asked me. Do you need me to stay or are you all right?"

"I'm fine now."

"Well, anytime you need me, you call and I'll come."

She nodded, and he squeezed her hand, hating to leave her but he wanted to find out more about Steve Douglas's trial.

A few hours later he was working again. He decided to drive by and check on Macy just to be sure everything was all right after their long afternoon at her family's grave site. As he drove down the street all was quiet, but he felt his senses go on high alert. Suddenly, a shrill, ear-splitting howl seemed to be coming at him from all directions.

An alarm!

An alarm was going off somewhere on this street. He stopped in front of the Lassiter house where the noise was the loudest. Someone was trying to break in. He swerved into the drive. The entryway light was on and the front door closed. The noise stopped and the sudden silence was almost as shocking as the noise had been.

Nick jumped out of the car and ran toward the house. The porch light came on. He ran up the steps and Macy opened the door. She stood before him wearing a robe, hair tousled and carrying a cane like a weapon. Her eyes were wide with fear.

Nick, one hand on his gun, looked around before entering the house. "You all right?"

"Something set off the alarm." Her voice quivered.

"Yeah, I heard it. The neighbors did, too. Most of

them are out on their porches. I'll let them know you're okay."

He stepped out on the porch and waved before examining the door and pointing to the sharply etched fresh scratch marks on the door frame.

"You think someone was trying to get in?" Her voice trembled slightly.

"Someone was *almost* in," Nick replied. "That's probably what set off the alarm. I'm guessing he had the door partially open when it went off like that. I told you the neighbors here keep a close watch on each other. He only had a few seconds to run for cover before everyone was awake and out their front doors."

Nick called the station to report the disturbance and received permission to handle the investigation, then turned to Macy. "Let's sit down and talk for a minute. Give you a chance to calm down." And give him more time to look at her. Even dressed in a dark green robe of some kind of silky fabric, that fiery hair tumbled around her shoulders and no makeup, she was beautiful.

They sat down in the living room and Nick glanced around, taking notice. This stately old home had been the scene for a lot of violence. He intended to bring that to a close if it was at all possible. And with God's help he believed it was.

Now that things had calmed down, Macy looked worn out. He could imagine what waking up to the sound of that alarm going off could do to a person. No wonder she was slumped in the chair, eyes closed. He fought the urge to wrap her in his arms, holding her close, comforting her, but this wasn't the time to allow personal emotions to distract him. Right now he could serve Macy better by keeping focused on what had happened here tonight.

His heart clenched at the thought of what she'd been put through, and he hadn't been here to protect her. He couldn't watch over her every minute of the day and night, but he still felt guilty. "You all right?"

She opened her eyes and gave him a faint nod. "I will be, as soon as I pull myself together. Nick, what do you suppose is in this house someone wants badly enough to break in?"

He didn't want to answer that, mainly because he thought this intruder might have been after *who* was here, not *what*. He had a bad feeling that someone wanted to eliminate the woman who was keeping everything stirred up.

Nick shook his head. "I don't know, Macy. I'd guess it might be something valuable or even incriminating. We'll just have to keep searching and pray we find it before the intruder does."

"I know, but it's so frustrating. I did have a flash of something. I guess you'd call it a memory. It was a voice—a voice I felt I'd heard before, but it was loaded with hatred."

"What did it say?"

She cleared her throat, looking shaken. "You brat! Get away from me."

He listened while she repeated the remembered words. While it wasn't much, he'd file it away with the other bits and pieces they were accumulating. Maybe it would all fit together eventually.

"You thought it seemed familiar?"

"Yes, but only for a minute. I wasn't exactly hearing it, you know, just remembering someone saying it. I have no idea whose voice it could have been."

Nick didn't want to go there. For his money it had

probably been a remembered echo of the killer's voice. And who would have sounded more familiar than her father, the man who had gone to prison for killing his wife?

He reached for his flashlight. "I need to look around outside. Lock the door behind me."

Nick left the porch light on and stood looking around. A small piece of mud lay about a foot from the door, but he didn't see anything else. He turned on the flashlight and descended the steps, checking the ground in front of the house. Then he walked slowly around the side of the building, searching for footprints or anything out of order, but didn't find anything. Back in front again, he stepped up on the porch and Macy opened the door. He shook his head, answering her questioning expression. She still looked shaken, but she moved aside so he could enter.

He patted her shoulder. "How about making a pot of coffee, and let's talk."

Nick watched as she went through the motions, noticing how the simple, everyday task seemed to calm her somewhat. He sent up a silent prayer of thanks that Joe had fixed the alarm and installed new locks. Instead of sitting here watching her move around the kitchen, he could have been investigating a fatal crime scene.

The thought of something happening to Macy sent a surge of concern through him. Although he hadn't known her very long, he couldn't bear the thought of losing her. Somehow he had to learn what was going on, and figure out a way to keep her safe. It all kept coming back to that. He had to keep her safe.

When the coffee had perked and she'd warmed cinnamon rolls in the microwave, they sat down at the table. Nick waited until he thought she had settled down to something approaching normal before bringing up what had happened. He didn't want to point out what could be the reason for tonight's activity, but he couldn't neglect to warn her of the possibility, either.

"Okay, now. Someone wants something that is in this house. He'd tried to break in before you came. But now, you're in the way of him finding it. He can't very well break in during the day because someone would see him. So we have to consider the fact he might be trying to get rid of you first."

Macy stared at him, looking shocked. "Me? You think someone tried to get in...to kill me?"

He nodded and she stared at him, mouth open. Finally she said, "I suppose you could be correct. Which only shows I'm on the right trail. That someone else must have killed my mother."

"Possibly. And then again, maybe it has nothing to do with your mother. We don't know who or what is involved at this point, and we can't jump to conclusions. Why don't you go to a motel for the rest of the night? I don't want to leave you here alone."

"I won't be alone. I'll call Hilda. She said she'd come anytime I needed her."

Nick nodded. "Call her now."

Macy frowned at him. "No, I'm not calling her. I just said that to make you stop. I will not have you making decisions for me."

"I'm not trying to make decisions for you. I'm trying to keep you alive. You might show some appreciation."

She got to her feet. "I think you'd better leave."

"I think so, too, before this goes any further. You follow me to the door and make sure it's locked." He whirled and left the room, leaving her to trail along behind him.

She stopped at the door, looking up at him, as if regretting the way she had acted. He gazed down at her and his heart clenched. "Look, Macy, something serious is going on, but right now we don't know what. It started after you arrived and it seems to be centered on you."

She stared up at him, mouth open and eyes wide, her expression revealing just how vulnerable she really was.

He wondered if she could see how reluctant he was to leave. "I hate to go, but I have to. I don't have a choice. Things are under control right now, but keep this door locked and don't be too quick to trust anyone. You call me if anything doesn't seem right."

He patted her shoulder, and she nodded. He repeated, "Anything. I don't care how minor it seems. You call."

She gave him a shaky smile, and he turned and walked out to his car, hating to go. At least the alarm was working all right, and after he reported in at the station, he'd make it clear to Sam that he was concentrating on this neighborhood for the rest of the night.

If anything else happened, he'd be here—to keep Macy safe. What he felt for Macy went beyond wanting to help her. He finally faced the truth. He was falling for her.

TEN

After he left Macy's, Nick drove to the station to finish reporting about the break-in. Before he'd gotten downtown Sam was on the phone, demanding he check in. If he was in trouble, he had a good idea why. Macy Douglas.

He couldn't stop thinking about this case. And the way he felt more connected to the copper-haired woman than just wanting to solve the mystery. Yes, he wanted to find the persistent intruder, but his strongest desire was to free Macy from her past in that house. She would never be able to move on until she learned the truth.

And ye shall know the truth and the truth will set you free.

The Bible verse flickered through his mind and he prayed it would work out that way. If the evidence proved Steve Douglas was guilty, he wasn't sure Macy could handle it. She was so convinced of her father's innocence there didn't seem to be room for any other alternative.

Nick also knew if she ever reached the place where she could move on, he wanted to continue being a part of her life. He'd never felt this way about a woman before, but Macy had walked into his life, into his heart, from the moment he had seen her in the shadowed yard of the old Douglas house. Everything had moved so fast, he still didn't know how it had happened. He just knew that it had. And he wanted it that way.

Sam glanced at him. "You get the problem at the Douglas house taken care of?"

Nick nodded. "Someone tried to break in and it set off the alarm."

"Any idea who it was?"

"No one saw anything and evidently he ran off before I got there. But there were scratch marks on the door and the alarm alerted the neighborhood."

Sam leaned forward and folded his arms on the desk. "I'm getting a lot of pressure from Garth to back off with this Macy Douglas thing."

Nick eyed him for a minute. "Any idea why he would care?"

"No, but I've been thinking. It happened a long time ago. No reason I can see for Garth to get all shook up over it. After all, it didn't concern him then, and I can't see why it would now."

Nick shook his head. "It did concern him. According to you and some others I've heard talking, it cost him the election. I've heard he took it pretty hard."

Sam nodded. "You're right on both counts. But Steve was arrested for killing Megan. They're both dead. So why's he so upset now?"

Nick hesitated, and then decided to bring it up. He had a hunch that was what Sam wanted. To get it out in the open. "Because Steve Douglas might not have been the real killer. Maybe it was someone else. Someone close to Garth Nixon."

"Or maybe even the guy himself?" Sam asked, one

eyebrow quirked. "Is that what you're thinking? You've been working on this behind my back, so let's talk about it."

"I'm not ready to point fingers at any certain suspect, but someone is trying to prevent Macy from finding out anything about that night. So I'm guessing whoever it is has something to hide."

Sam nodded. "Sounds like it. You got anything definite to go on?"

"No, but did I tell you someone left Macy a picture of her father wearing prison clothes and a threatening note stating that if she kept on with what she's doing she'd deserve whatever she got?"

Sam leaned back and crossed his arms. "Uh-huh. Seems like someone might be getting a little worried. I can see why. You get away with a crime for seventeen years and then someone comes along trying to end your party. Reason enough to worry, I'd say."

Nick eyed Sam. There had to be more to this little meeting. "So you think Garth might have something to hide?"

Sam heaved a sigh. "I don't have any idea. Thing is, Garth was good to me when I was in college. I didn't have all that much and he gave me some money. Not a lot, but it helped. And he had a hand in getting me this job. Talked me up all over town."

"I see. So what are you going to do?"

The police chief looked at him for a minute, then gave a resigned sigh. "Well, I didn't want to get involved in this, but I can't see a way out. I guess I'm going to do all I can to help you find out the truth. That's the oath we took and it's the job we do. I don't want to live with the knowledge that I let a killer walk free, even if it turns out to be someone who did me a favor."

Nick nodded. "I'm thinking we'll get it done, too. You can only hide murder for so long. After a while people start talking."

Sam picked up a ballpoint pen and examined it before looking up at Nick. "Okay, we're in, even if it ends up costing us our jobs. And it very well could."

Macy parked in front of Benson and Associates and sat staring at the front of the building, running over the list of questions she wanted to ask Raleigh Benson, and wondering if she could trust his answers. Finally she got out of the car and approached the building. The young, dark-haired receptionist smiled at her, large golden hoop earrings swinging against her cheeks. "May I help you?"

"I'd like to see Mr. Benson, please."

"Do you have an appointment?"

"No, but ask if he can talk to Macy Douglas for a few minutes." What would she do if he said no? Surely he would want to see her, try to talk her into leaving town if for no other reason, since that seemed to be a personal quest of his.

The receptionist came back, smiling. "Mr. Benson will see you. Right down that hall, first door to the right."

Macy paused in the doorway of the office. Raleigh sat behind a large oak desk with matching oak bookcases on either side of the window. He looked at her, his eyes narrowed so all she could see was a suspicious gray glint.

"Miss Douglas?"

"Good morning, Mr. Benson. I'm sorry to bother you, but I need to ask you something. Since I'm new in town,

I don't know very many people, and you *were* my grand-mother's attorney."

He bent his head in agreement, but didn't say anything.

Macy took a deep breath and continued. "It concerns my father's newspaper business and my mother's dress shop. Since they're both deceased, whatever happened to their property?"

Raleigh Benson stared at her for a minute, then he said, "Your father's name was on the dress shop title along with your mother's. He had it put on the market and it sold right away. The proceeds paid for his lawyer. The newspaper was sold by the bank to pay off his debts. The house, by the way, was free of debt, and since Opal soon moved in and lived there, it remained in the family."

Macy sat silent, trying to take all of this in. Her mother's business was sold to pay for her father's lawyer? Something occurred to her. "Who was his lawyer?"

Again Raleigh didn't answer right away. Finally he said, "I was."

This was the man who had supposedly defended her father? What kind of job had he done? "So I'm guessing you charged a good-size amount for your services, even though your client went to prison."

He answered forthrightly enough. "I only charged for the time I actually put in working on the case. If you're thinking I cheated your father out of any money, I can assure you that's not true."

"I want to see the papers concerning both transactions. Where will I find them?" She waited to see what he would say. Had he handled the sales of the properties? She hadn't thought of that earlier.

He kept eye contact with her, his expression set in granite. "I'm getting the idea you don't trust me."

Right. He could bank on that. At the moment, she could count on the fingers of her right hand the names of the people she actually trusted, and Raleigh Benson wasn't one of them. "I haven't been overwhelmed with people welcoming me to town, and the comments about my father, and about me, haven't exactly inspired trust."

He moved a small bronze paperweight of a pacing lion a few inches to the right. "I know it probably seems strange to you, but people in this town have long memories. I realize it's been seventeen years, but for some of us, it's as alive as if it were yesterday."

Macy eyed him thoughtfully, wondering where he stood in the fracas. Did he support her father or did he believe Steve Douglas was the murderer, and how much would that have affected the way he defended his client?

Raleigh rested his arms on the desk and leaned toward her. "You know, you look a lot like Megan, and I'd guess you have her fire. She was a good businesswoman, owned one of the better shops in town, and she was free from debt. I have a hunch she's the one who paid off the house you're staying in. Steve liked money and what it could buy. He wasn't interested in saving it, though."

Macy bit back the words she wanted to say. This wasn't the time to let her resentment of his derogatory comments about her father get in the way of trying to pry information out of him. He had known them both. Surely he would have had some idea of what had happened that night.

"I don't remember anything about either of them or what they were like." Every time she said those words they hurt just a little bit more, no matter how many times she repeated them.

Raleigh looked surprised. "Nothing? You don't remember anything at all about them?"

Was that compassion she saw in his eyes? Not something she would have expected from Raleigh Benson. "I have dissociative amnesia. I'm hoping living in that house will jog my memory and help me recall something…anything…about them."

"I see." He looked thoughtful. "That would make a difference, wouldn't it? You were there. Knocked out and lying at the foot of the stairs. But you have no recollection of what happened? Amazing."

She changed the subject. "You were my father's attorney. Just how hard did you work at trying to save him, anyway?"

He looked at her for a minute before nodding. "I knew from the first time you walked into this office you would be trouble."

"What kind of trouble?"

"Stirring things up again. Look, I did my best for Steve, but we lost. That's all I have to say about it."

"You mean you won't answer any more questions?"

"Not at this time." He glanced at his watch. "Now, if you will excuse me, I have an appointment due in a few minutes. I'm afraid I'll have to bring this conversation to a close."

Macy wanted to refuse to be dismissed like this, but then she reluctantly rose. "Very well, but I may have some more questions later."

He didn't answer, just stared at her. She shrugged and walked out of the room. She had a curious feeling, as if she'd said something closer to the truth than she had suspected, and he was wondering just how much she knew.

That afternoon she was sitting on the porch about an hour before dark when Nick drove in. She hadn't heard from him all day, which was unusual.

He climbed the steps to sit down in the other wicker chair. "You doing okay?"

"I guess so." As okay as she could be considering everything that was going on. However, she enjoyed having him to herself for a little while, liked the way his eyes lit up when he looked at her, too. He smiled and her heartbeat accelerated, pounding so hard she could almost feel it thumping against her chest wall. Why did he have this effect on her? She'd never felt this way about any other man.

She was aware the way she felt about him went much further than just friendship. Something she hadn't counted on. She'd tried to avoid it, but it seemed that the harder she tried to hold him at arm's length, the more she felt drawn to him.

Nick watched Macy, noticing the signs of stress in the way she moved her shoulders, the way she grasped the arms of the chair, and how she kept tightening her lips and staring out at the street. He had a hunch living here was getting to her. Which wasn't surprising, considering the nonstop effort someone was making to get rid of her. He admired her courage and her determination, but he couldn't stop worrying about something happening to her. She was so vulnerable, yet so stubborn, and she didn't have anyone else. Just him. That worried him. What if he slipped up some way? Thinking about it was keeping him awake at night.

"Has anything else happened that I don't know about?"

"Not that I can think of. I'm still going through the house, trying to find information that would throw light on my parents' lives back then, but so far I haven't found anything. I know it's been seventeen years since they lived here, but there should be something pertaining to them. I mean, their clothes are still here. Why would anyone have discarded records and personal papers?"

Nick shrugged "I don't know. Maybe it's all packed away somewhere. Keep looking, and if you need help with it, call me."

He wanted her to ask him to come inside and help right now, prolong the time he could spend with her and maybe accomplish something at the same time, but since she didn't, he changed the subject. "Have you remembered anything more?"

This wasn't something he was really comfortable with. He knew she needed to get her memory back, but this was unfamiliar territory for him. And there was always the chance that her memory would return at the wrong time, putting her in more danger. Since they had no idea whom they were looking for, she might trust the wrong person and confide in him—or her. The intruder might be a woman for all he knew.

Macy shook her head, "No, and it's so frustrating. I thought all I would have to do was live here and it would all come back to me, but it's like that part of my life is just gone and I can't call it back."

Nick reached out to take her hand and she curled her fingers around his. "Don't give up, Macy. I really believe at the right time it will all come back to you."

He didn't tell her of his fears that someone would do

everything possible to prevent that. She had enough to deal with, but he would do some heavy-duty praying about it. God would keep her safe. He had to. Because Nick was starting to realize how bleak his life would be without Macy.

They talked a little longer, and she told him about her visit with Raleigh Benson. Macy paused. "There's something about him that strikes me wrong. He doesn't want me here. When I first met him he kept trying to get me to sell the house and got upset when I refused. And he said something today that bothered me. He said the minute he saw me he knew I would be trouble. He acts friendly until I cross him and then he gets frustrated. And he's made it clear he wants me to get out of this house and leave town."

"So something's going on there. I guess we add him to our suspect list."

"Add whoever is calling me. In fact, I think that person belongs at the top."

"Do you recognize the voice?"

"No. But it sounds strange, like the guy's using something to disguise it."

There were products on the market that would work with the telephone to change the caller's voice. At least three types that he knew of. There were the stand-alone ones, about the size of a deck of cards; there were the phone-integrated voice-changing devices; and there was even a software-based one. They could change the voice's speed, change the gender, even add background noises. He needed to check into that.

"So you might recognize it if he spoke normally. Which means it could be anyone."

Macy sighed. "And that puts us right back at the beginning. We really don't have any strong leads."

Nick leaned forward, elbows resting on his knees. "I had a talk with Sam. He's come over to our side. It's a legitimate investigation now, with the police department working on it with us. Just give us time, Macy. We'll get to the bottom of it. We've got a good bunch of men out there looking for evidence."

Nick wasn't as confident as he sounded, but she had enough to worry about. He wanted to ease her mind a bit if he could, but he could tell from her expression it wasn't working. She'd shown too many times that she didn't have any confidence in the police. That's probably what she was thinking right now. "Look, Macy. I know it looks hopeless, but there's someone out there who knows the truth."

"Yes, but they're not coming forth with any information we can use."

"We'll find them. Keep praying and have faith. Something is bound to break before long."

"I know, but the person who made the phone call knows I'm here. What if he's watching me, knowing what I'm doing, and I have no idea who he is? He could be standing beside me in the supermarket, and I wouldn't even know it."

Yeah, he'd thought about that. The person harassing her had to be Megan's killer. Who else would put so much effort into trying to drive her out of this house? And that would mean that Steve Douglas hadn't killed his wife.

Which brought him back to the problem of what the police had done all those years ago. No matter how hard he tried, he couldn't get away from it. Joe Tipton had been sure they hadn't really tried to find out the truth. So if someone else had killed Megan, could he clear Steve Douglas's name without tarnishing his own father's reputation? Surely it wouldn't come to that. Either way, he had to take care of Macy. He'd reached that decision, accepted it and moved on. Both their fathers were dead. Macy was alive. Whatever it took, he had to keep her that way.

"You need to be extra careful, Macy. I'll do my best, but I can't be with you all the time. Stay around people. And don't trust anyone."

She gave him a serious look. "Anyone?"

He grinned. "Well, you can trust me. But be careful around anyone else. And keep my phone number with you all the time. You call and I'll be here as soon as possible. And that's a promise."

She nodded. "I'll do my best. But we both know if someone wants to get to me, he probably will."

"But we're going to do everything we can to prevent that."

His cell phone rang and he answered to find Sam on the line. "Yeah, I'm on my way. Just got delayed a little. Be right there."

Nick hung up the phone and looked at Macy. "I should have been at work a half hour ago. Are you sure you're all right with staying here by yourself? Don't think you have to if you're afraid."

He hated to go, knowing she'd be here alone. It got harder every time. He'd sleep on the porch just to make sure she was safe if she'd let him, but she'd probably call Sam to make him leave. It was hard to take care of a woman who wouldn't cooperate. "I'll drive by occasionally and check on things. And now that Sam's agreed to an open investigation, we need to think about putting a trace on your phone line."

She stared at him, looking surprised. "I never thought of that. Can you take care of it for me?"

"Sure I can. I'll get right on it, and if you're uneasy about anything, you call me, okay? And keep me up to date on anything you find out."

He stood there, smiling down at her, but there was worry in his eyes. Macy realized she was getting so close to him she could do a fair job reading his expressions. She kept telling herself to back off, but she had to admit she really didn't want to. Not when the sight of him sent her heart racing.

"Look, Macy. I'll do everything I can for you. I promise you that," he said before departing.

She nodded. Nick was the one person in this town she believed she could depend on.

After he left, Macy went back inside. She paused at the entrance of the living room, playing over in her mind what had happened here seventeen years ago. It would have been night, the lights on. She would have been upstairs in bed. Asleep? Maybe, maybe not. She closed her eyes, trying to summon the memory.

She had come downstairs, had stood here in this very spot, looking in. Macy didn't know how she knew that— she just knew. She caught a glimpse of the room in the mirror over the fireplace, as she had done that night. She'd been so scared, so horrified by what she'd seen.

She stared at the fireplace. It was coming, she could feel it. Suddenly, in her mind, she saw one of the chairs overturned, lying on its side. The crumpled body of a woman lay on the floor, a dark blue robe twisted around her. Blood seeped from a head wound. A blue house shoe lay a short distance away.

Silence as thick and stifling as a heavy blanket smothered Macy. She struggled to breathe. A sound, half human, half animal, tore from her throat, ending in pain-filled words that were barely recognizable.

Mama! No! Don't hurt my mama!

Macy sank to the floor, overcome by the vividness of the memory. It slowly faded from her mind until nothing remained. The body was gone, the chair sitting erect. She slumped forward, head bent over her lap, tears flowing down her cheeks to soak the jeans she wore.

Her mother. She'd seen her mother's body.

Just the way she had seen it that night.

Finally she wearily got to her feet and climbed the stairs. As if on cue, the phone rang. Macy stumbled down the hall to her grandmother's room, her heart pounding in her throat. She held the receiver to her ear, noticing in an abstract way how her hand trembled. "Hello?"

The voice rasped over the line, harsh and distorted. "Getting ready for bed, I see."

ELEVEN

A chill swept over her. He could see her? "Why are you doing this?"

"I told you why. You're not wanted here. Pack it up and get out of town, or stay here and take what you get. It's up to you."

The line went dead, and Macy sank down on the bed, fighting for control. He was watching her. Even knew she was upstairs. Of course, the downstairs lights were off, except the one in the foyer, but he would have to be standing outside to know that.

She slowly pushed herself off the bed and crept down the hall to her room. Between the memory of seeing her mother's body and the emotions aroused by the phone call, she probably wouldn't close her eyes all night.

After she'd tossed for the better part of an hour, she finally drifted into a troubled slumber, dreaming someone was chasing her down a darkened street, while a harsh voice loaded with hatred echoed through her head. "Run, you brat! Run."

She woke the next morning feeling groggy, but managed to choke down a few bites of toast and strawberry jelly before Neva arrived. After getting her started cleaning upstairs, Macy decided to continue searching the lower rooms, hoping to stumble across something that would jump-start her memory. She started with the corner cabinet in the formal dining room, the room she never used, preferring the homier atmosphere of the kitchen. The top drawer held a collection of odds and ends, none of which seemed important. In the second drawer she found an envelope full of pictures that appeared to have been taken at a Christmas party.

There was her mother and her father. That child in the charming, long-skirted blue dress was her. Most of the people in the group picture were casually seated or standing, but one young blonde woman posed for the camera, chin lowered, lips pouting, and a sly glance slanted upward with an inviting expression.

She looked familiar, but Macy couldn't come up with a name for her. Somehow she didn't seem to fit in with the others. The longer she stared at the picture, the more uncomfortable she felt. As if she had known the blonde woman and hadn't liked her. She pawed through the rest of the drawers, finding nothing else. On an impulse she spread the pictures out on the kitchen table, planning to look closer at them later, maybe ask Hilda Yates about them. Since Macy had called to apologize, her grandmother's friend had made an effort to stay in touch, calling and dropping by occasionally. Hilda was easy to talk to, friendly and helpful. Not like Neva.

Today Macy had asked Neva what her mother had been like, thinking if she had worked for Megan Douglas she should have intimate knowledge. Neva had stared past Macy for a minute before speaking. "She looked a lot like you. People called her beautiful. She lived in this big house. She had everything she wanted."

Macy had watched her, waiting for something more

personal, but Neva had gazed into her coffee cup, not meeting Macy's eyes. "She had you."

Then she had just walked out of the room and started cleaning, leaving Macy staring after her. Neva could be friendly when she wanted to, but most of the time she just worked, not talking much. She seemed to miss Opal, though.

Today Macy had found her standing before the open closet in her grandmother's room. Neva had said she was thinking about Opal, remembering her wearing these things, just thinking about how hard it was to realize she was gone. She'd also noticed Neva didn't do much cleaning in that room, as if she were distancing herself from it. Like it hurt her to spend much time in it.

But at least Neva had memories of her friend. Macy had no such memories herself. All she could do was ask God to help her and pray that something would unlock her mind.

Something else bothered Macy. Neva had asked for a key today. Although Macy was sure it would have been all right, she'd decided against it.

This house was too big and too strange for her to feel comfortable, and she had enough to worry about without having her house key floating around out there. Not that she didn't trust Neva; she did, of course, otherwise she wouldn't have hired her in the first place. But that problem with the alarm had been a wake-up call. She'd be more careful from now on, more prone to watch her back.

Hilda knocked on the door, and today she brought brownies. She and Macy sat on the front porch talking while Neva worked inside.

Hilda nodded toward the car in the driveway. "That looks like Neva Miller's vehicle. What's she doing here?"

Macy leaned her head back against the chair and breathed in the scent of honeysuckle. "She came to the house looking for a job. Said she'd worked for both my mother and grandmother. So I took her on. Why?"

Hilda looked uncomfortable. "Nothing, I guess."

Macy gave her a stern look. "Oh, no, you don't. You had a reason for asking and I want to know what it was."

Hilda shrugged. "Yes, she did work for Opal. I was just surprised to see her here so soon after you arrived in town. Neva's had a hard life. Her daughter was kind of wild. She got in trouble and went to prison. Then when she got out she was killed in a car wreck."

"She told me her daughter had died, but I didn't know any of the rest. I guess that explains why I thought she was sort of odd. She probably didn't want to talk about it." Macy shook her head in compassion. Poor Neva. She was glad she'd hired her. She probably needed the money.

"Yes, she doesn't talk much about Lindy. In fact, she sort of keeps to herself. Oh, she goes to church and community events, but she doesn't really get involved."

"She works hard and the house looks better since she started taking care of it," Macy said. "Neva's not much for standing around talking. She gets the work done, and I like having someone besides me in the house. I'm still not used to anything this big and empty. Houses like this weren't built for just one person to live in."

Hilda laughed. "No, I guess back then they planned on big families to fill all of these rooms. These old mansions are beautiful, but I prefer something smaller, myself."

Macy hesitated. She needed to know something about the woman who had raised her the first seven years of her life. The mother she still couldn't remember.

"Hilda, I want to talk to someone who might have been a friend of my mother's. It's driving me crazy that I can't remember her. I need more than just a vague idea of what she was like. Who can I talk to?"

"You have to remember, Macy, that Megan was a lot younger than me. I was her mother's age. Opal's age. I didn't know her all that well, didn't know her friends, but I never heard anything bad about her and as far as I know she didn't have any real enemies. Oh, Anita bad-mouthed her every chance she got, but that's all."

"She had one enemy," Macy said. "The one who killed her."

Hilda nodded. "That's true enough. Someone did that. Have you found her diary?"

Her diary? Her mother kept a diary? It would be full of personal information. Things Megan Douglas had thought were important enough to record. No, she hadn't found anything like that while searching through the house. She stared at Hilda. "You mean she actually kept a diary? I didn't know that."

"Opal found it a couple of months ago. She mentioned it to me and said it hurt her to read it."

Macy felt as if someone had handed her a gift. Her mother had kept a diary? She had to find it. That hand-written account might be just what she needed to jog her memory.

"It was right after that she started acting funny."

Macy zeroed in on that comment. "Funny? How?"

Hilda leaned back, frowning. "Like I told you, she

started talking about Steve, and she never did that before. It was almost like she felt he was innocent."

She gave Macy an intent look. "Opal lived her beliefs. If there was anything in that diary that pointed to someone besides Steve, Opal would have done something about it. She'd have felt that was what God would want her to do."

Macy felt excitement building inside her. *God, help me find that diary. Show me where my grandmother kept it.* She was sure it held a clue to her mother's death, or at least she prayed it did.

Hilda glanced at her watch. "I need to go. Lila Vester is in a nursing home and I promised I'd stop by and see if she needs anything. But if this place gets to be too much for you, I've got an extra bedroom and you'd be welcome anytime."

Macy got to her feet, smiling. "I know that and I appreciate it. I believe meeting you was one of the nicest things that has happened to me since coming here."

And meeting Nick was another, but not something she felt like talking about, even to Hilda. She wasn't sure about what she felt for him. For the time being she was calling it friendship although she knew it went beyond that. But friendship was all she could handle right now.

After Hilda left, Neva stepped out onto the porch. "Was that Hilda Yates? What was she doing here?"

"We've become friends. She drops by occasionally."

"Where did you meet her?"

"At church. Do you go to church, Neva?"

Neva's face creased in a smile. "Yes, I go to the same church Hilda does. The church Megan and Opal went to. I saw you there the first day you came."

Macy tried to remember seeing her, but there had been too many people that Sunday, and after all, Neva had been practically a stranger then. "I'm sorry I don't remember. It was my first time there and I was a little overwhelmed."

"Oh, that's all right. I'm easy to overlook." Neva changed the subject. "I heard Hilda talking about Megan's diary. I knew she kept one but I've never seen it."

"Neither have I," Macy said. "But I'm going to start looking for it. If my grandmother found the diary and was troubled by it, then maybe she really was coming around to believing someone other than my father had killed my mom. You know this house better than I do. Would you have any idea where Grandmother Opal might have kept it?"

"No, but I'll be on the lookout for it. If you find it before I do, I'd like to see what she wrote. It would bring Megan back to me, just by reading her thoughts and what was important to her. It would be a blessing."

Macy nodded, but she had reservations about showing her mother's diary to anyone except maybe Nick. It would seem like a betrayal of her mom's private thoughts and feelings. If she found the diary, she'd read it and then decide if it had any bearing on their mystery. If not, she would keep it to herself.

Neva left and Macy made a run to the grocery store to pick up a few items. After she got back home, she sat down at the table to look at the photo album from her grandmother's room, hoping she would see something familiar. The pictures of her with her parents were heartbreaking, but from what she could see there had been love, laughter, life. Nothing that pointed to problems.

Nick tapped on the door frame of Sam's office. "You got a minute?"

"Sure. What's on your mind?"

He stepped inside and sat down. "I want to run something by you. It's this Megan Douglas thing. There's no evidence that she got involved in politics like Steve did. She ran her own business, raised her daughter, went to church. I can't find anyone who had a problem with her, except maybe Anita Miles, and I don't have anything that points to her as a killer."

Sam shook his head. "Anita's a hard one to handle when she's upset about something. But we need more than the fact she didn't like Megan. Megan was a good woman, but she had a reputation for being kind of outspoken and she ran a tight business, didn't put up with much. I remember she fired an employee for stealing. Can't think of the name right now, but it's a little farfetched to think someone killed her over something Steve did."

Nick shifted his weight, trying to get comfortable. "Yeah, I thought of that. A killer's mind doesn't usually work that way."

"You had any luck turning up anything about Steve and that so-called affair Anita is always ranting about?"

"No. In fact, from what I've learned Steve Douglas was a family man. He worked late at the paper sometimes, but not very often. Mostly he was home in the evening."

Sam looked at him, nodding as if that was no more than he had expected. "We need to check into that alibi of his. He was supposed to have gotten a phone call about a wreck outside of town. When he got there nothing had happened. Maybe someone set him up. Let me get his file and see what they learned back then, or if they bothered to follow through."

He walked over to the file cabinet, opened a drawer

and thumbed through it. While Nick watched, he went through it again and then turned to face him with an incredulous expression.

The file was gone.

Nick was bewildered. He'd read through that file, taking notes, but not finding anything that pointed to evidence being mishandled by the police. He'd put it back exactly where he'd found it. And now Sam was looking at him, frowning.

"You can drop what you're thinking, right now. Yes, I've been reading the file, but I put it back. If it's missing, it's not my fault. Someone else has it."

Sam didn't look convinced. "Who else would be using it? You're the one obsessed with this case and digging around on your own."

"I have no idea, but I'd like to find it, too. I've still got a few questions about how the case was handled."

Sam eyed him, skeptically. "I'd hate to think one of our guys took it, and I can't see why they would. After all, none of them were involved in police work back then. They were too young."

Nick shrugged. Sam didn't seem to have any problem believing he took it. "Well, I hope you find it. I'm going to check on Quent. He's the one who told Macy her dad was having an affair with Anita."

"Yeah. I guess Anita testified to that at the trial, but I never put much stock in it. Any man who had Megan wouldn't waste time looking at Anita. Even back then, she was trouble."

"That's what I heard. But it won't hurt to check it out." He got to his feet. "I'll let you know how it turns out."

Nick drove to Quent's and pulled into the driveway of the white frame bungalow where he lived. Soon he was settled in a brown leather armchair that looked almost as old as the house.

"Good to see you, Nick," Quent said after they were both seated. "What's up?"

"Oh, not much. Macy told me what you said about Steve and Anita. You really think something was going on there?"

"Well, I don't have any proof one way or the other, but my gut feeling says no. He already had a good woman. Megan Douglas was a fine person, hardworking, everybody liked her. Never could figure out why anyone would kill her."

And that was the problem, Nick thought. No one, except Anita, seemed to have anything against Megan. Maybe he needed to take another look at Anita. He'd always felt she was more talk than action, but he'd been wrong before.

"What's Anita's problem, anyway?"

Quent was silent for a moment, looking thoughtful. "Well, mostly, I guess, she thinks she's so important that no one should cross her and she should have exactly what she wants. No one is supposed to get in her way."

"Yeah, I suppose that's right. I've pretty well tried to stay away from her. She's usually on the warpath about something."

"Yeah, someone isn't doing things the way she wants and she has to straighten them out."

"But what does that have to do with Steve and Megan Douglas?"

"Steve was a good-looking man. Lots of women had their eye on him, but when he met Megan, the search was over as far as he was concerned. I never heard of him looking at another woman once they started keeping company."

"And Anita didn't like that, I guess."

"That's right. From what I heard she did everything she could to break them up, but she just couldn't do it. That testifying against him was probably her idea of getting even."

"I think you just gave Anita a reason to commit murder."

Quent nodded. "I wouldn't take her off your list."

After he left Quent, Nick decided to drop by and see Macy. He knew he was probably overreacting, but he couldn't stop worrying about her. Something just didn't feel right.

TWELVE

The doorbell rang and Macy answered to find Nick standing there. It gave her a warm feeling, knowing he cared enough to be so protective. Not that she needed it, of course; she could take care of herself...but still, it was nice.

He grinned at her. "Thought I'd drop by and see if I could get a glass of tea or something."

She laughed. "There's a pitcher of tea in the refrigerator and Hilda brought over a plate of fresh-baked brownies. Will that do?"

"Sounds great. Lead me to it."

Impulsively, she caught his hand and strolled with him toward the kitchen, strongly aware of the way he walked so close to her. Macy knew she needed to think less about Nick and more about the quest she had embarked upon, but her heart wasn't listening.

He pulled out a chair and sat down at the table, as casually as if he belonged there, and for a fleeting moment she wished he did. Macy acknowledged to herself that she was being foolish. Nick Baldwin was a policeman working to unravel this case. If he was friendly and protective, it was merely because he was that kind of man.

A man a woman could trust and depend on. She hadn't met many like that. But he hadn't given any indication of wanting to be more.

Nick moved the photo album over where he could see, and Macy drew up a chair beside him, enjoying the intimacy of sitting so close together while they looked at the pictures. He pointed at one of her and her parents. "That must have been taken at the park."

Macy shook her head. "No, we'd been fishing."

She glanced at him, wide-eyed, not sure where that had come from. How could she know where they had been? Yet she did. Knew it as surely as she knew her own name.

Nick stared at her. "You remember it?"

Macy looked at the picture, then back at him, unable to hide her confusion. "No. It just slipped out. I don't really remember anything about it."

"Maybe that's the way it's going to be. Not one big flash of memory, just little things."

She hoped it wouldn't be that way, although recent events seemed to bear it out. "I'm too impatient for that. I need to know. I have a feeling we're running out of time, like something is about to happen. Something bad."

Nick had a serious expression, and she could see the concern in his warm brown eyes. "Has anything new happened since I last saw you?"

Macy hesitated, not sure how he would take this. Finally she took a deep breath and nodded. "I don't know how this will sound, but the other day I was in the living room, and something happened. In my mind I saw one of those gold brocade chairs turned over on its side, and then I saw my mother's body lying in front of the fireplace."

She couldn't tell from Nick's expression what he was thinking, but she wouldn't blame him if he thought she was losing it. Why should she expect anyone to believe something so strange? It was time to step back and stop trying so hard, put it in God's hands and trust Him to work it out for her benefit. A difficult task for someone who always had to be in control.

After a long, drawn-out moment, Nick asked, "What did she look like?"

Macy stopped to think. "She had on a blue robe. One shoe was lying over at the side. She was facedown on the carpet, and her head was all...bloody. That's all I remembered before it faded, like everything else has done."

Nick sighed. "I've never had to deal with anything like this before, so I'm not sure what to think about it."

"I'm not, either," Macy confessed. "But it was so vivid that I have to believe I'm remembering it exactly the way it was."

"So, you believe it was a memory. Something you'd seen before and it just came to you."

"Yes, that's exactly what I think. In fact, I'm sure of it. What else could it be?" Macy didn't know if Nick believed her, but at least he appeared to be seriously considering what she had said.

Now he looked thoughtful, eyes narrowed, lips pursed. "Why don't you write down what you remember every time it happens? Write it all, every detail. You never know when some simple thing might turn out to be a good clue. And we need all the help we can get."

Macy nodded. "All right. I'll make a record of what I've remembered in the few days I've been here."

She wondered how he would take what she planned to ask next. "Who was the chief of police back then?"

Was it just her imagination, or did his expression change? Some subtle shift that seemed to signify tension. She waited for his answer, which seemed slow in coming.

"Clyde Jackson. He's Garth Nixon's cousin."

"His cousin? The chief of police was the cousin of the man who hated my father? Maybe my grandmother Douglas was right. The police might not have looked too hard for a killer when my father made such a convenient scapegoat."

Nick just looked at her for a minute, and she felt a strangeness come between them, like an invisible barrier. As if he was hiding something. Was Nick holding something back—something she needed to know? Had she been too quick to trust him?

"Maybe so, but I'm not finding any evidence that points to anything like that."

"I think it's there. We just haven't found it yet." And yes, she was being stubborn, with nothing to back it up. Call it a hunch, or call it just plain bullheadedness, but she couldn't believe her father had received a fair trial. The more she learned about it, the more she believed that someone had worked hard to see that her father went to prison for a crime he never committed.

Nick watched her, knowing exactly what she was thinking. He didn't tell her his father had been a policeman back then because he wasn't sure how she would react. He didn't want anything to come between them, but he couldn't betray his father's memory, either. The man he knew and loved would never have taken part in a conspiracy to send an innocent man to prison. He'd try to consider both sides, but he hadn't come up with any information pointing to his father and until he did, he'd keep on believing Angus Baldwin was innocent of all charges of corruption.

How did he get into a situation like this? He was just beginning to understand what a storm this woman could stir up. Enough to turn Walnut Grove on its ear, just as she had threatened to do when they first met.

"Look, Macy. It's too early to jump to conclusions. We need to go slowly, examine every piece of evidence. Not be too quick to zero in on anyone." In an investigation like this where there wasn't any clear indication of what happened or who did what, it would be easy to take off in the wrong direction. They needed to be careful.

From her expression, he had a hunch *careful* wasn't on her agenda right now. She shot him a look that plainly said she wasn't in a mood to slow down the investigation. She wanted action and she wanted it this instant. He could understand that, but he also knew if she was too impatient she could destroy what little evidence was out there, and not even know it.

She firmed her lips, then said, "I'm not trying to railroad anyone. I just want the right person caught and made to pay for his crime. But if the police or anyone else took part in a cover-up and my father went to prison because of it, I want them brought to justice, too."

Nick could understand how she felt, and he was going to do everything in his power to help her, but he was praying his father had nothing to do with whatever had happened with Steve Douglas. If Macy knew his father had been a policeman, she'd probably stop trusting him altogether, and he wanted to avoid that.

So right now he needed to change the subject before she started wondering why he wasn't jumping in to agree with her about the police. He needed to keep her as far away from that subject as he could while he dug a little deeper. He wanted to talk to someone who might have a fair, unbiased attitude. Hard to find someone like that in this town.

Another thing he wanted to do was take a look at the old crime photos of Megan's death and see if they matched what Macy claimed to have to seen. He wanted to believe her, but stuff like this was way out of his league.

They talked a little longer, then Nick left, planning to drop by the police station and see what new information he could learn. Sam was out, so Nick sat down at his own desk and pulled up the crime scene photos. The photos were old, but good. He clicked through them, then jerked to a stop. Wait a minute. What was that last one? He backed up, staring in disbelief at the body of a woman lying in front of a fireplace, the same fireplace where Macy claimed to have seen her mother's body. The woman wore a blue robe, one shoe was off, and a chair was overturned, exactly the way Macy had described.

The hair on his arms furred. This was scary. He had assumed Macy might be getting her memory back, but he hadn't expected this exact copy of the scene. Nick stared at the picture, feeling helpless. He just might be in over his head on this one.

Macy wandered back to the table, deep in thought. Nick seemed reluctant to discuss any questions about the police and how they had conducted their investigation back then, which bothered her. Not that she was fully convinced they had done something wrong, but she wanted to know for sure.

She closed the photo album and started to gather up the pictures she'd left on the table when something struck her. She shuffled through them again. One was missing. Macy spread them out on the table, looking closely at each one. The picture with the arrogant blonde woman was gone.

She paused, thinking back to when she'd last seen it. Had it been here when Neva left? She couldn't remember if Neva came to the kitchen before leaving. Had Nick taken it? Why would he do that? Surely she would have seen him carry it out with him. Or had someone come in while she was at the grocery store?

She had the new locks, the alarm…no one could get in. Right? A shiver of fear rippled up her spine. Had someone managed to get a key, after all?

Would she ever be safe in this town?

A folded piece of paper fell out of the handful of pictures she had scooped up. She didn't remember seeing it earlier. Macy dropped the pictures and reached for the piece of paper, wondering where it had come from. She was sure she hadn't overlooked it.

She unfolded the paper, staring in shock at the words written there.

This is your last warning. Get out while you still can.

THIRTEEN

The next day, Nick drove by the Douglas house hoping to find Macy at home. On opening the door she greeted him with a smile that warmed his heart. It seemed as though she got more beautiful every day. They went to the kitchen as usual, settling at the table with cups of freshly brewed coffee. Today she wore a blue T-shirt and jeans, her hair hanging loose around her face. She smiled at Nick and he grinned, relaxing and enjoying the moment. Life didn't get much better than this. What a shame it couldn't be this way all the time.

He pulled himself together and handed her the sheaf of papers. She accepted it and raised her eyebrows at him. "What's this?"

"A transcript of the trial. I want you to go over it, looking for anything that doesn't sound right. Just glance through it a couple of times, taking notes if you think something seems a little off, or if you have a question."

Macy took the papers and thumbed through them, her expression intent. Nick leaned back in his chair, watching. She glanced up at him, smiling her thanks. "I'm glad to have this. I've wondered about the trial. But I warn you, I'm coming to this with my mind already made up.

I believe he was innocent. I'll try to be fair, but I can't turn off the way I feel."

"I understand that, and I don't want you to. Read through it, mark the places where you have a question, take notes. I'll do the same, and so will Sam. Then we can put the three together and see what we come up with. You might catch something I won't, and I might see something that wouldn't mean much to you. Have you had any luck looking for the diary?"

Macy shook her head. "No, I've searched, but a house like this has a lot of hiding places. Neva's looking, too, but so far we haven't found anything. I'm reasonably sure if it's here I'll find it, because I won't stop looking until I do."

Nick nodded. That was no more than he would expect from her. She never gave up. But he had a feeling she might be taking on more than she could handle. "Did I tell you that I was talking to Sam and he got up to get the file on your dad's case and it was missing?"

"Missing? You mean it was misplaced or what?"

"I mean it was gone. We haven't found it yet, so I'm assuming it's not at the police station. No one seems to have seen it, which isn't surprising since it's an old file and there's no reason for anyone to have it out looking at it."

"But you have no idea when it disappeared? So it could have been gone for a long time. Wonder what happened to it."

Nick heard the skepticism in her voice, as if she didn't believe him. Like she thought someone, maybe Nick, had hidden the file so it couldn't reveal information about her father's arrest. So she still didn't trust him. He was surprised at how much that hurt. What would it take for her to realize he was on her side?

"No, it hasn't been gone very long. I'd been looking at it recently, but I put it back where it belonged. I'll keep searching for it, but it might have gotten tossed out by mistake."

She just looked at him, not even bothering to answer, which upset him even more. She might as well call him a liar and be done with it. "Look, Macy. No one in the police department took that file, if that's what you're thinking."

"And I'm supposed to believe someone from outside walked into the police department and took that certain file and walked out with it, and no one saw them? That doesn't speak very highly of our police force, does it? And how would that person know where to find the file in the first place?"

"I'm not trying to convince you of anything. I just mentioned it, and I wish I'd kept quiet. You've already convinced yourself the police are guilty, but in an investigation, it's a good idea to keep an open mind. You can overlook important clues otherwise."

She stared at him for a minute, and he could see she was trying to get herself under control. He needed to do the same. Sounding off at each other would get them nowhere.

After heaving a sigh, she started talking. "Look, Nick. I'm sorry if it sounded as if I was blaming the police. It's just that I don't know what to think and it all seems to be closing in on me. Very few people want to help and some of them, like Anita and Garth Nixon, are verbally attacking me whenever I see them. It's wearing me down."

He could see that, and maybe he needed to calm down a little. "I can understand. It's getting to me, too. But don't give up, Macy. Keep trusting God, and have faith He'll help us learn the truth about it all."

Macy changed the subject. "The other day when we were looking at the photo album, did you happen to see a few photographs spread out on the kitchen table?"

Nick stopped to think. "I may have, why?"

"Oh, nothing probably."

"No, that doesn't work. You brought it up. So start talking."

She shrugged. "I had some pictures I'd found in the corner cabinet and I meant to look at them later, so I left them on the table. One picture showed a group of people. My mother and father, and me, and I didn't recognize the rest. There was a blonde woman who seemed to think she was something special. Something about her looked familiar, but I couldn't remember who she was. When I was getting ready to shut up the house for the night I put the pictures away, and noticed the group picture was missing."

"Missing? So you think someone took it?"

"I don't know. You evidently didn't take it, Neva says she didn't, I was upstairs part of the time when she was here and then I went to the grocery store. Maybe someone came in and took it. But there was a threatening note in it." She got up and walked to the cabinet and brought it to him.

He read through the note and looked up at her. "This was in with the pictures?"

She nodded. "It wasn't there earlier, but when I started to put them away I found it."

"Are you sure Neva didn't take the picture?"

"Why would she want it, and if she did, why would she lie about it?"

He didn't have an answer for that, but he'd rather believe Neva took the picture than to think someone walked in and left that note, or even worse, entered the house after it was locked.

"Could I look at the rest of pictures? Maybe I'd know some of the people."

She got up and walked to the corner cabinet, returning with an envelope of photos. Nick spread them out on the table. Pointing to the people he recognized and calling them by name. Macy leaned over his shoulder and he could smell her perfume, something light and spicy, making his senses reel.

Nick forced his attention back to the pictures. "I can't see anything here that would be important enough for anyone to take. Wonder why someone would want that one and why leave a threatening note?"

Macy slumped down in a chair across from him. "I don't know. But I really think someone took it. I just don't have any idea who it could have been."

And that worried him. She didn't have any business staying here by herself. Didn't she have any idea what it would to do him if something happened to her? No, probably not. After all, he'd never given her any reason to know.

"Look, Macy, you have to keep that door locked at all times. You're keeping things stirred up, I'm running around asking questions and someone could be getting very nervous. You're the key to this thing, and whoever it is, he has a strong reason to silence you."

He could see the fear in her eyes, and something else.

Anger. Macy Douglas was a fighter, and he loved her all the more for it.

Nick stopped to think about that. Love? All right, he'd finally admitted it. What he felt for Macy was the kind of love a man and woman could build a life on. He wasn't sure how she felt about him, but he knew for sure how he felt about her. This was the wrong time to tell her, though. First he had to figure out a way to keep her alive.

Nick placed his hand on her shoulder, wishing he could take her in his arms and keep her safe, but he knew she would never really be safe until they had unraveled the puzzle of what had actually happened in this house that night.

"Keep in touch, okay? And if anything looks just the little bit wrong, call me."

She nodded. "I will, and thank you for all you've done for me, Nick. I appreciate it."

"No problem."

He smiled down at her, thinking how vulnerable she was. He'd check back later, just to make sure she was all right. It seemed that he was always walking away from her, but what else could he do? He couldn't learn anything sitting here. If he was going to solve this case he had to get out and do some investigating. The fact that it was an old case closed out years ago wasn't helping. But if there was anything to be found, he'd find it. He had to. Both he and Macy were too personally involved to just turn their backs and forget all about it. There was too much at stake.

Nick had been gone only a few minutes when Hilda Yates dropped by. They sat in the living room and Macy thought about how nice it was to have one friend in this town who would stop by just to visit.

Hilda sat down in the chair and stretched out her legs. "So how have you been getting along?"

"Okay, I guess." Macy hesitated, then decided to go ahead. "Hilda, my grandmother Douglas always believed there was something rotten going on with the police department concerning my father's arrest. That they knew he was innocent but they arrested him and let a killer go free. Did you ever hear anything like that?"

Hilda looked thoughtful. "You know there was some talk about it, but I guess most of us just thought it was some of the political junkies stirring up trouble. Tell you what, why don't you ask Nick? His father was a policeman back then."

Macy stared at Hilda, feeling as if someone had just knocked the breath out of her. Nick's father was a policeman? Why hadn't he told her? She'd mentioned this to him a few times and he'd brushed her off, even defended the police. In fact, he had gotten upset when she questioned his version of the missing file. Just when she thought she'd found someone she could trust, she learned he'd been deceiving her the whole time.

"You mean Nick's father might have been part of the cover-up concerning my parents? He certainly never mentioned to me his father was with the police. Wonder why?"

Hilda swung her head around to look at her. "Now, Macy. Get that look off your face. Nick had nothing to do with what happened back then. He was just a boy."

"No, but I've brought this up, and he just sort of ignored me, pushed it aside. Maybe his father was involved. I believe Nick Baldwin has some explaining to do."

Half an hour later, Hilda left, still protesting that she was sure Nick hadn't been trying to hide anything from Macy, and stressing that she was sorry she had brought it up. Macy let her go without arguing, but she had something to discuss with Nick Baldwin. If he came by this afternoon, the way he usually did, he was going to tell her about his father, whether he wanted to or not.

She spent the rest of the day alternately working herself into frenzy and then attempting to calm down until she heard what Nick had to say. The trying to calm down part didn't seem to be working well so far.

When he arrived shortly after he got off work, she met him at the door. She'd listen to what he had to say, but it had better be good. "Let's sit out here."

He raised his eyebrows, and she knew her tone of voice and probably her expression had warned him that something was wrong. She took a chair, and waited until he sat down before starting in. "Hilda was here today."

"Oh?" He looked wary. "That's nice. Is that what got you riled up?"

She pinned him a straight look. "No, I told her that my grandmother thought the police were involved in railroading my father, and she just happened to mention that your father was a member of the police force back then. Funny you never bothered to bring it up."

His expression turned thoughtful, and he nodded his head. "I figured that would come up sometime. I didn't mention it because I wanted to see what I could find out first."

"And did you find anything?" Macy heard the skepticism in her voice and knew he caught it, too, but she didn't care. Right now she felt betrayed by someone she was beginning to believe she could trust. She watched as he shook his head.

"No, not yet, but I'm still looking. If it's out there, I'll find it."

"I don't doubt it, but will you make it public, or will it just be your little secret?"

He stared at her. "Is that what you think of me?"

"Right now I don't know what I think. If you were playing it straight it seems like you would have told me the truth."

His expression hardened. "Why would I do that? You obviously had already decided that anyone connected with the police department was corrupt. Would you have been willing to listen to reason?"

Macy stiffened. "I am a reasonable person. I believe I'd have listened."

"Not if it concerned your father, you wouldn't. You have your mind made up and you've found the police here guilty without any proof. Well, this is my father, and I have a right to defend his memory just like you do with yours. If I learn he was involved in any kind of cover-up, I'll tell the truth. Until then I won't listen to anyone run him down."

She stood up. "Fine. I believe we understand each other. I'll keep searching for the truth, and if it involves your father, so be it."

Nick got to his feet. "That works for me. I'll keep looking, too, and if I find your father was guilty, that's the way it will be."

He strode down the steps and toward his car.

Macy stared after him. What had she done? She should have been more polite, more subtle, instead of behaving as if she thought he had deliberately lied to her. But then on second thought, he hadn't been honest. He had hidden the truth from her, knowing how she felt.

Nick Baldwin had betrayed her. He deserved every word she had said, and more.

So why was she crying?

Nick sat in his living room with the TV blaring the evening news, not really hearing or seeing anything on the screen. Hands wrapped around his coffee mug, he stared blankly into space, reviewing his confrontation with Macy in his mind.

He understood how she felt, understood her blind, unswerving devotion to her father, but he couldn't betray his father, either. Before he could bring accusations against his own kin for anything, he had to have proof. Yes, his dad had been a policeman, a good one. None better. He'd stake his life on that. Angus Baldwin had left the police force the year after Megan Douglas was killed.

Nick paused, struck by that. Why had his father stopped being a police officer? Did it have anything to do with Megan's death? Three years later his father had been killed in a sawmill accident. Nick was sixteen years old, and he could still feel the agonizing pain of losing the man he'd loved and looked up to.

He turned off the television and stepped out on the deck, staring up at the sky. A full moon showered the world with silver light. Stars gleamed in a dazzling display. A soft breeze brought a hint of honeysuckle. He stared at the beauty of the night, knowing he was in over his head. This case was turning way too personal. Was his love for his father blinding him to reality? Could the police actually have been playing dirty back then? No, he couldn't believe it. Wouldn't believe it without absolute proof. To do otherwise was totally unthinkable.

What would he do if he actually turned up the proof? Could he indulge in his own cover-up? No. He couldn't. Nick sent a silent prayer upward. *God, help me learn the truth about what took place back then, no matter how much it hurts.*

He wished nothing had happened to stir up this mess. But then he wouldn't have met Macy. Just knowing her, being with her, had enriched his life more than he would have believed possible. And now they were in danger of being torn apart by the secrets of their past. Somehow he had to unlock those secrets, find out exactly what had happened, including the parts both their fathers had played.

Nick leaned on the railing, staring at the shadowed yard, praying God would show him the way. He couldn't afford to make a mistake. If he was the one who turned up evidence proving Steve Douglas had killed his wife, he could lose Macy…if he hadn't already. No, he couldn't let that happen. She was right. He should have told her the truth earlier. Somehow, he'd make it up to her.

Something sailed past his head, thudding on the floor of the deck. Nick dropped to the floor, reaching automatically for the gun he'd left in the living room. A rock lay about two feet away from him with something tied to it. He reached for the rock, closing his hand around the rough exterior. His pocketknife made short work of the string, and he unfolded the paper, reading the scrawled words.

If you're smart, you'll stay away from Macy Douglas. I don't want to hurt you.

FOURTEEN

Macy threw back the covers, unable to sleep. She kept seeing Nick's face, hearing the things he'd said…and the way she had reacted. She understood how he must feel about his father, but she had a father, too, one who had died in prison.

She wandered through the upstairs, lonely and a little intimidated by the silence. The house was more familiar now, but she still didn't feel completely comfortable here, especially at night.

Macy paused in the doorway of her parents' room, thinking about going in, then changed her mind and moved on to Grandma Lassiter's room. Nothing in there held her interest, so she stepped down the hall to the child's room, the room that had been hers once upon a time. Back when life was good, and she was a young girl wrapped in her parents' love.

The phone rang, and she rushed back to Opal's room to answer. "Hello?"

Silence.

She tried again. "Hello?"

A long pause, then a voice, harsh, contorted, sounding not quite human, rasped in her ear. "Two women died in that house. You'll be the third."

"Who is this?" Macy demanded.

Click.

Macy sat on the bed, holding the receiver, too stunned to replace it. Two women. And she'd be the third? So were the two women her mother *and* her grandmother? Did that mean her grandmother hadn't died a natural death, either? Had there been two murders in this old house?

Who had been on the other end of that call? As always, the voice sounded strange, as if something had been used to disguise the sound of it—so she wouldn't know who was harassing her. Which probably meant the caller was someone she'd met and whose voice she would recognize.

According to Nick, some of the techniques available could even change the gender of the voice. So was her caller a man or a woman? Now she wasn't sure. Who did she know that would do this? Anita Miles? Macy could see her making the calls. She was arrogant enough to think she could get away with anything. Even murder? Quite possibly. And yes, Anita's name was on her list.

Macy finally went back to her room, not to sleep, but to lie awake staring at the ceiling, going over the names of the people who might have a reason to make threatening phone calls to her. The list was too short for comfort, but her mother's killer would be the one with the most to lose. It was time to stop worrying about the political end of things and concentrate on who had a reason to kill Megan Douglas.

She needed to go deeper, talk to people who had known her mother, find out more about her life here. The problem was finding people who wanted to talk to her. Most of the people she'd met either didn't want to get involved or turned on her for being her father's daughter.

God, help me, please. I don't know where to turn, what to do next. I'm just stumbling in the dark. She'd driven Nick away and now God was all she had left to rely on. The danger she faced was too real, too terrifying. If God didn't help her, she wouldn't survive.

Midmorning, she was sitting at the kitchen table reading the trial transcript again, hoping something would jump out at her. Something that would point away from her father. She wished Nick could be sitting at the table with her so they could share thoughts, but for now that was out of the question. Without him her life seemed so empty. But he didn't want anything to do with her now.

Neva entered the kitchen, and Macy stared at her in surprise. "The door was locked. How did you get in?"

Neva smiled and shrugged. "I found an extra key the other day. I didn't think you'd mind if I took it."

Macy looked at her, stunned. Hadn't she refused to give this woman a key when she asked? What was this all about? And the only spare key was in the top drawer of her father's desk where she had placed it. Had Neva been going through the drawers?

"Look, Neva. I'm still getting used to this house. It makes me nervous for anyone to be able to just walk right in. How about giving that key to me. I'll be here to open the door whenever you arrive."

And what was she doing here, anyway? It wasn't her day to clean.

Neva stared at her, not saying anything.

Macy held out her hand. "The key?"

After a moment Neva held out the key and Macy took it, hoping she hadn't made extras. Why was she so determined to have a key? Did she have one before? But then the old one wouldn't work on the new locks.

"Look, Macy. I didn't mean anything wrong with the key. I really had forgotten you were still nervous about being here. To tell the truth, I don't blame you. The house is too big and too quiet. I understand completely."

"That's all right, Neva. Maybe someday I'll be more comfortable here." When her mother's murderer had been caught and brought to justice. "This isn't your day to clean. Did you need something?"

"No, not really. I just thought I'd help you look for that diary. I'd like to see it, like to read what Megan wrote. We both lost something the day she died. You lost your mother, I lost a good friend."

Macy tried find the right words to say. She didn't want Neva helping her look for the diary. Whatever was written in those pages was private, her mother's musings about the things that mattered to her. She wanted to read it first. Not with Neva or anyone else looking over her shoulder.

"No, that's all right. I'm not in the mood to look today. Maybe later."

Neva finally she nodded. "All right. It was just a thought. I'll see you on Friday."

Neva left and Macy spent the next two hours hunting for the diary, but didn't find anything.

Nick decided to drop by and talk to Clyde Jackson, the man who was chief of police when Megan Douglas was killed. He found Clyde puttering in his garden. "You got a minute? I'd like to ask you about something."

Clyde motioned to a bench under a large oak tree.

"Sure. Glad to take a break. I'm getting too old to work for very many hours at a time. Can't do what I used to do."

They sat while Nick tried to think how to start without upsetting Clyde. He wanted information, so it would probably be better not to come on too strong. "You know Macy Douglas is in town?"

Clyde nodded. "Heard she was. Heard she was stirring things up a bit, too."

"Yeah. She believes her father didn't get a fair trial. That he was innocent of killing his wife. You got any thoughts on that?"

Clyde sat silent looking at him. Finally he said, "You asking if there was any dirty work going on?"

"Something like that." Okay, there it was. Would Clyde get mad and order him off the property, or could they just sit and talk in a reasonable manner?

For a minute Clyde didn't say anything, then he shrugged. "I always figured this would happen one day. But it's been so long, I'd sort of thought maybe no one would bother to check into it."

Nick's heart sank. Was he saying it was true? This wasn't what he wanted to hear. He wanted Clyde to deny any possibility, but it didn't sound as if that was what he was going to get.

"What do you mean?"

Clyde scuffed the ground with the toe of his shoe for a minute, not replying, while Nick waited impatiently. Finally he shrugged. "The early signs pointed to Steve. His alibi didn't hold up and Anita was running around telling everyone she was having an affair with him and that he was talking about getting rid of Megan."

"What about later signs? Did you do any real investigating?" Surely they did. That was their job.

Clyde took a deep breath. "You got to remember Steve had been pretty rough on Garth. Family stands up for family, and Garth's my first cousin. And no, I hate to admit it, but I didn't look all that hard for any conflicting evidence."

"You didn't try to find anyone else who might have done it?" Nick shook his head, not wanting to hear this. His stomach churned at the thought. "You just stopped looking?"

Clyde nodded. "That about sums it up. I've never felt right about it, either. Particularly since Steve died in prison. Megan Douglas was a fine woman. She didn't deserve what was done to her, and neither did that little girl."

Nick didn't want to ask the next question, but he had to know, for his own satisfaction if for nothing else. There had been too much secrecy. It was time he found out the truth, and the former chief of police was the man to tell him. "My dad was a cop. He probably worked on the case."

Clyde shook his head. "You thinking he did anything wrong? You can forget that. Angus was a straight arrow. Deacon in the church. He wouldn't take part in anything like that."

Nick slumped against the seat, relief surging through him. This was what he needed to hear. He had been right to believe in his father. He'd known it all along. The man he'd looked up to had been true to his beliefs, just the way he'd taught his son to be.

Clyde stared out at the garden and Nick could see from his expression he was struggling with something. He waited, wondering what was coming next.

"I need to get something off my chest. Guess now

is as good a time as any. I didn't do Angus right. He wasn't sure Steve was guilty and I was still upset over what Steve had done to Garth, him being family and all. I know he's not worth much, but I didn't realize that back then. And like I said, family stands by family when you can."

He stopped talking, staring out over the neat rows of garden plants before giving a sigh that seemed to come from his toes. "Me and Angus had words over it. I made it kind of rough on him, and he finally quit the police and went to work at the sawmill. That's where he was when that stack of logs fell on him. I always felt like it was my fault he got killed. If it hadn't been for me, he'd probably still be a cop."

Nick stared at him, overwhelmed by what he was hearing. He'd lost his father and had spent the rest of his life missing him. Now he had to listen to this? Words, boiling hot, clogged his throat, almost choking him. He clamped down on them, struggling to hold those hateful statements inside. His father wouldn't want him to take his anger out on Clyde.

Neither would God.

Clyde watched him, his expression showing understanding and compassion. "I know you can't forgive me, so I won't ask you to, but I've regretted it every day of my life. That's why I quit police work. Didn't have the heart to run for office again."

Nick stared at the ground, fighting for control. *God, help me. Don't let me lose my temper and say words I shouldn't.*

He took a deep breath, trying to hold his voice steady. "I can't forgive you right now, no. Maybe I can someday, but not right now."

"I understand and I don't blame you. I'd feel the same way if I was in your shoes. You're working on this case, trying to find out what happened. If there's anything I can do to help straighten out this mess, let me know. I'd like to get the truth out there. One more thing, Nick. Be careful around Garth. He's my cousin, but I don't trust him very far anymore."

Nick forced the words out. "I understand he was in Jefferson City at the time Megan was killed."

Clyde nodded. "That was the story, but Tim Dawson insists he saw him that night, right here in Walnut Grove. I never saw him myself, so I can't say, but I've learned not to put anything past him. And I hate to say it, but it's a good thing he lost that election. We've got too many crooked politicians. We don't need another one."

"You think he could kill someone?"

Clyde hesitated. "I don't know. I guess we never know what we can do until we've done it. I'm not ready to point fingers, but I guess I wouldn't put it past him. Garth always thought he was a little more important than anyone else, that we owed him. I don't think he'd stop at anything to get something he thought he deserved."

Nick absorbed this, knowing he felt the same way about the man. He needed to find out more about Garth and some of the things he'd done. If he'd stepped on enough people, someone should be willing to talk.

He stood and looked down at Clyde. "Thanks for letting me know my dad wasn't involved in anything out of line. I couldn't believe he would be, but there were all of those rumors floating around."

Clyde nodded. "He was a good man, a good policeman. Better than I was. Look, Nick. I mean it. If I can help bring this to a close and find out the truth, just tell me. I'll do all I can."

"It might help if you'd go back over everything you can remember about what happened. You might come up with something we could use."

"I'll do that," Clyde promised. "I'll be in touch."

After leaving Clyde, Nick wanted to tell Macy what he'd found out, but he didn't think she'd believe him. Besides, he was still upset about both what he'd learned from Clyde and the disagreement he'd had with Macy. The more he thought about it, the more it disturbed him. Sure, he understood how she felt about what had happened with her parents, but she should have realized that he cared about his father and his father's reputation, too. She could have cut him a little slack.

Still, he had to admit that he missed her. He'd give anything to sit down with her and talk about what they'd learned. And not just talk about the past, but just talk, like two people who cared about each other. He missed the light in her eyes when she was excited, the warmth of her smile, the way he felt just looking at her, but it might be best to give them both time to cool off. He didn't want to stir up another argument.

Nick stopped in front of the newspaper office. This wasn't anything he looked forward to, but it had to be done. Garth Nixon had been at the center of the controversy stirred up by the political editorials written by Steve Douglas. So it was time to talk to Garth and get his side of the story.

He got out of the car and walked inside. Bess Underwood at the front desk looked up and smiled at him. "Hello, Nick. What brings you this way?"

"I'd like to talk to Garth if it's okay." And if it wasn't, he still planned on talking to him.

"Sure. Go on back. He's in the second room on the left."

Nick stepped behind the counter and walked in the direction she had indicated. He doubted if Garth wanted to talk to him, but that was okay. It wasn't as if the guy had a choice. He was here, and he had some questions to ask.

Garth looked up with a surprised expression when Nick entered his office. "Nick? What are you doing here?"

"Just wanted to talk. You know Macy Douglas is in town?"

Garth frowned. "Yes. I'm aware of that. Why?"

"You know she's trying to learn what happened on the night of her mother's murder. She doesn't believe Steve killed Megan."

"It doesn't make any difference what she thinks. There was a trial. A jury said he was guilty. In my opinion, he got just what he deserved."

"I heard you were out of town when it happened, but then again, it seems someone saw you here that night. Which is correct?"

Garth gripped the pencil in his hand so hard it broke in half. "What difference does it make where I was? No one ever suggested I had anything to do with Megan Douglas. I wouldn't have wiped my feet on her. My gripe was with Steve."

"I was a kid then. But from what I hear Steve came down rather hard on you in the newspaper."

Garth's face flushed with rage. "He ruined my life. I had a chance to win that race, then he started writing those editorials. Turned people against me. He cost me the election for no reason except he belonged to the other party."

Nick pressed a little harder. "You knew them both. Who would have a reason to kill Megan?"

Garth shook his head. "I have no idea and I wouldn't tell you if I did. No one gives a rap why Megan was killed or who did it. Megan wasn't as important as she thought she was, but she did serve a purpose. Her death and the trial got rid of Steve."

Nick left the newspaper office, convinced Garth Nixon knew more than he'd admitted. It was obvious the man hated Steve Douglas. He didn't even try to hide it. A hatred that strong would be difficult to control. On the other hand, there wasn't any evidence that really pointed to Garth. That was the trouble. They didn't have evidence that pointed to anyone except Steve. And that so-called evidence was awfully weak. There had to be more, and somehow he had to find it. Before the true killer could strike again.

Hilda dropped by and she and Macy sat on the front porch, which seemed to be more comfortable for Hilda. Macy knew Hilda missed Opal a lot and she had a feeling the front porch wasn't quite as personal as being inside the house where her friend had lived.

They chatted about trivial things for a few minutes and then Hilda turned serious. "Look, Macy. You're wrong in the way you're treating Nick. He didn't talk to me about it, I heard from someone else, but you're not being fair."

Macy bristled at her words. How did she get to be the one in the wrong, and what business was it of Hilda's or anyone else? "I don't know what you're talking about."

"Yes, you do. And I want to assure you that no one who knew Angus Baldwin could think he would be involved in any kind of cover-up. And you ought to know Nick would believe in his father, just the way you believe in yours."

Macy sat silent, knowing that was too close to the truth to be comfortable. Although she hated to admit it, what really hurt was that she knew Hilda was right. What she couldn't say out loud, because it was too personal, was the way the days seemed long and impossibly dreary without Nick dropping in occasionally. She missed his smile, the way he could cheer her up when she was feeling discouraged, missed him in more ways than she could count.

"You don't understand."

"I most certainly do. You and Nick are coming at this from different directions, but you both want the same thing—to learn the truth about what happened and how it involved your parents."

Hilda changed the subject as if giving Macy time to think about it. "How are you getting along with Neva?"

"All right. I feel very sorry for her."

"Yes, you have to feel sorry for her. Some people can handle trouble, some can't. Neva has a hard time dealing with the problems life has hit her with."

"Does she clean your house?"

Hilda shook her head. "No, I clean my own. I can't afford a housekeeper. Besides, even though I feel sorry for her, I'm not all that fond of Neva. She's got a short fuse. Doesn't take much to set her off."

Macy thought about that. How had her grandmother gotten along with the housekeeper? "Did Grandmother Lassiter have a run-in with Neva?"

Hilda laughed. "Opal never had a run-in with anyone. Not like Megan. No one ran over *her*. But from what I picked up, Opal was thinking of getting someone else to clean her house."

"Why was that?"

"I have no idea. Opal was rather picky. Maybe Neva was slacking off on the job or something. I know Opal would want it done her way. Have you had any more trouble with Anita?"

"Not yet, but I wouldn't put anything past her." That woman was walking trouble on the hoof.

"Neither would I. Watch your back where she's concerned. And as usual, if you need me for anything, you call me."

Macy promised, knowing she wouldn't be likely to call. Her problems were her own, and since they might turn dangerous, she wouldn't want to involve Hilda or anyone else.

Hilda left and Macy went back inside. She paused, staring up at the staircase, the way she did every time she stood here, waiting for a memory that never came. Would she remember anything else? The silence overwhelmed her, but nothing happened. As she stood listening, a scratching, rasping sound pinned her to the floor. What was that? Someone—something in the house?

Macy stood frozen, straining to hear. The sound came again—from the living room. She tiptoed toward the doorway, striving to be quiet. A quick glance revealed an empty room. The sound came again, from the window behind the love seat. She crept forward, heart pounding, determined to see what was going on.

FIFTEEN

When she was halfway across the room a stick rose into sight scratching on the window. Someone was making that noise.

Macy rushed toward the window just in time to see someone whipping around the corner of the house. She ran to the kitchen window, but no one was in sight.

Why was someone working so hard to drive her from this house? And would she live long enough to find out?

Later, Macy thought about what Hilda had said concerning Nick. She really should call and apologize. Maybe she would do that later today. Right now she had some questions for attorney Raleigh Benson.

She drove to the office not sure if he would talk to her again, but she was ushered into his office with no problem. Macy sat down across the desk from him and decided to demand some answers.

"I'd like to know why you don't want me in that house. Why you want me to sell it."

He frowned. "Why would I care where you live? And as for finding a buyer for you, I was simply trying to help."

Okay, let that one go.

"I've been reading the trial transcript. The evidence

against my father was very flimsy to say the least. If you're such a great attorney, why couldn't you get him off?"

He sat in silence, and then after a moment he shoved his chair away from the desk and got up, moving to gaze out the window with his back to her. She was getting ready to demand he turn around and look at her when he started talking.

"You're right. I didn't really work that hard to help your father. I was angry at him for the way he had treated Garth Nixon, and I had a feeling he was actually guilty of killing his wife."

"If you weren't going to defend him, why did you take the case? And it sounds like you let your politics get in the way of defending an innocent man. That's contemptible."

"Yes, it is. But Garth had promised me a job on his staff if he won the election. I was going through a rough time. My wife was sick. Medical bills were piling up and my son was into drugs. I wanted that job. I needed it. But I was a fool to trust Garth. I'd know better now."

Macy stared at Raleigh's back, willing him to turn around and face her, so she could tell him what she thought of the things he had just said. He had let an innocent man go to prison over a job. No matter how badly he needed it, how could he justify his behavior?

Raleigh continued. "I never should have been Steve's attorney. There was evidence against him, all right, but not a lot. If I'd done my job the way I should have, I probably could have got him a better deal. The jury found him guilty, mostly on Anita's testimony, I think."

Okay, she had to ask, even though she wasn't sure

she wanted to hear the answer. "Was my father having an affair with her?"

He turned around and looked at her, and she was stunned by the compassion in his expression. "I don't know for sure, but I doubt it. Anita is a piece of work. She wanted Steve. He didn't want her, and she couldn't handle it. Some people like Garth and Anita believe they're so important they deserve everything they want. They're both trouble. Stay away from them."

She couldn't believe his sudden honesty. "So she probably lied and let him go to prison. I understand she hated my mother, too."

Raleigh nodded. "Apparently so. That's what I've heard, anyway. But don't go jumping to conclusions. Just because they didn't get along doesn't mean Anita killed her."

"Well, someone did, and I'm sure it wasn't my father. I thought you and Garth were friends."

"Not any more. Garth likes to walk on the wild side and I don't want any part of that. I messed up once because of him and I've had to live with it. If you're successful in proving Steve was innocent, then I'll know for sure what I've come to suspect. I let him and Megan both down. What can I do to help you?"

Macy wasn't sure she could trust him, but he was her best chance at learning new information. "Would it help if you reviewed the evidence again?"

"It might. I'll pull it up and see what I can find out."

"I'd appreciate it. Will you let me know if you learn anything?"

"Yes, and I'll make sure Nick knows, too. Whatever the truth is, it's time we got some answers."

Macy left his office, feeling encouraged. As soon as

she reached home she headed for the living room, pulling out her cell phone. She had to restore her relationship with Nick. Her step quickened, even as she prayed God would give her the right words to say—and that Nick would listen.

She'd punched in half of the numbers of Nick's cell phone when the doorbell rang. Frustrated, she ended the call and marched to the front door. This had better be someone she wanted to talk to. She needed to call Nick before she lost her nerve.

She swung open the door and stepped back, surprised to see Nick standing there. He nodded at her, his expression serious. "May I come in?"

"Oh. Yes, of course. Sure." Macy clamped her mouth shut before she could babble any more. Why did this man have such an effect on her? Just seeing him like this, unexpectedly, turned her into an emotional wreck.

He entered, looking down at her, and she motioned toward the living room. "Let's sit down."

Regardless of why he was here, she was going to apologize. She had to do it not only for Nick, but also for herself. It was only right. Besides, she needed him. Needed to work with him, to learn what he had found out. She tried to ignore the fact that she needed him even more on a personal level. That was something she'd have to deal with later, but right now she had more important things to concentrate on.

He waited, eyebrows raised in a questioning manner. Macy took a deep breath and began. "I was out of line the other day. I realize you loved your father the same way I loved mine."

She stopped to think about that. Yes, she had loved her parents. She hadn't been sure about that before, but from living in this house, she had gradually come to know more about the relationship among them. At least she had received one benefit from being here. There had been love. Not only her parents' love for her, but she was confident they had loved each other.

Nick sat quietly, just looking at her, and Macy heaved a sigh. She was trying to make amends. He could at least act interested. "Look, I shouldn't have been so quick to jump to a conclusion about the police. I don't have proof anything was off center with them, but my grandmother Douglas was so sure, and you have to admit there was some room for doubt. It wasn't just something I made up."

He nodded. "Yeah, well, before this goes any further, let me say that I was too quick to fly off the handle, too. The fact is, we both had fathers, they're both gone. It's normal that we would want to defend them from any hint of wrongdoing."

"I realize that, and I'm trying to apologize here." And heavy going it was, too. If she had known it would be this hard, she'd have kept her mouth shut.

Nick grinned. "And I'm trying to tell you that we both need to apologize, so let's call it done and move on. I've got something to tell you. I wasn't sure how it would go over, but now I think it will be all right."

It was Macy's turn to wait. She wondered what he had in mind, but whatever it was, she would listen to the end instead of interrupting him with her own version of the facts. Right now it was enough to be sitting here with him again, seeing the seriousness of his expression, the curve of his lips...

She jerked herself up short. This wasn't the time to

be thinking like that. She needed to get her emotions under control.

Nick leaned forward, resting his arms on his knees. "I dropped by to talk to Clyde Jackson. He was the chief of police here when all this happened. He's also Garth Nixon's cousin."

"And you wonder why I've been thinking something fishy is going on?"

He held up his hand. "Wait, then you can talk all you want, but I'm going to get this out in the open, so just try to have patience."

Macy frowned at him, but she had to admit he had a point. And what had happened to her vow to be quiet and listen? The last thing she wanted to do was start another battle between them.

Nick waited a minute and then continued. "He admitted that he didn't try to find anyone else. The evidence pointed to Steve, and he was still upset over the editorials your father had written and the fact that Garth had lost the election. He says it has bothered him ever since."

"And you believe him?" She wasn't gullible enough to accept anything said by someone who had helped send an innocent man to prison. If it had bothered him so much why hadn't he come forth and told the truth years ago?

"Yes, I do. You didn't see or hear him. I did, and I believe he was telling the truth."

Macy pressed her lips together, determined not to say anything more until she heard him out. Let him convince her, if he could, that this Jackson could be trusted. She wasn't all that gullible. Nick could give him the benefit of the doubt if he wanted to. She needed proof.

Nick waited, apparently giving her time to respond,

before going on. "He said Garth was family, and you stood by family. Sound familiar?"

Macy nodded. Both she and Nick were committed to family—that was part of the problem—but that was beside the point. Police corruption was something else again. "So Clyde Jackson put his cousin ahead of doing his job. Is that what you're saying?"

"That about covers it. He did mention Anita and the things she was saying, and that there was evidence that pointed to your dad. But he also said neither you nor your mother deserved what had been done to you, and he offered to do anything he could to help."

"And you think we can trust him?" She could feel Nick watching and tried to calm down. If she wasn't careful she'd drive him away again, and she didn't want to do that. She clamped her lips together, asking God to help give her patience.

Nick watched Macy, realizing she was upset. He wasn't sure how she would accept what Clyde had said about his father, but he guessed he might as well try. If she took it the wrong way, he'd have to deal with it. "He said some things about my father, too."

Macy raised her eyebrows. "Oh, really? What?"

"According to Clyde, my father didn't like what was going on. He tried to do something about it, and Clyde admitted he made it so rough on Dad he finally left the police force and started working at the sawmill. That's where he died. A stack of logs rolled and fell on him. I was sixteen years old. I've missed him every day since then. Clyde said he had always felt it was his fault."

Macy stared at him for a moment with a compassion that almost undid him. After a long pause, she asked,

"You mean what happened that night cost both of us our fathers?"

Nick hadn't thought of it that way, but he realized she was correct. They had both paid a high price for something they had nothing to do with. "I guess that's right."

Macy looked thoughtful. "Which gives us an even greater reason to learn the truth. You think we can do it?"

"I'll bet we can. Working together and with God's help, we'll be a tough team to beat." She sat looking at him with those sea-green eyes and he wanted to take her in his arms and tell her it would be all right. But before he could follow through on that idea, she started talking.

"You know, Raleigh Benson said almost the same thing when I saw him."

Nick sat up a little straighter. "You talked to Benson? What did he say?"

Macy shrugged. "He admitted he could have done more to help my father and could probably have gotten him a better deal. He said Garth had promised him a job on his staff if he was elected. He was going through a hard time and he wanted that job."

"So he didn't work too hard to get Steve off, I guess." How could these guys live with themselves, knowing they had let an innocent man go to prison? They hadn't even tried to find the murderer. Just turned their backs and let him walk free so they could get back at Steve Douglas for writing those editorials. And they had thought that was all right? Didn't they have any sense of right and wrong?

"Is that all he said?"

"He's supposed to go over the evidence, looking for

anything that might point us in another direction, and he said he'd be in touch with us."

"I see. Well, maybe they both mean it. And I guess he did have a hard time back then. His son was on drugs. I believe he died of an overdose. I think that was his only child."

"He didn't tell me that. And his wife was sick back then. I don't want to feel sorry for him, but when I hear things like that, I just can't help myself."

Nick grinned. "You know what? We've pretty well eliminated two of our suspects. Maybe if we keep on like this we can find the killer because he'll be the only one left."

Macy smiled and patted his arm. "It's good to have you back on a friendly basis. I've missed you."

The touch of her hand was warm, intimate. It was good to be sitting here with her again. Hopefully after this they could keep their emotions under control and work together. At least he wouldn't be torn apart, thinking his father might have been involved. He felt better over that.

"I've missed you, too. We'll have to see that nothing else comes between us." And friendly wasn't what he wanted. He had more of a permanent relationship in mind, one that involved the two of them growing old together. This wasn't the time to talk about it, but he'd hold that thought and do what he could to make it a reality.

Macy's eyes twinkled with humor. "I think that's a good idea. I'll try to be a little easier to get along with, and not be so quick to mouth off."

Nick laughed. "I like a spunky woman. You say whatever you want to. I'm big enough to handle it."

That was one of the many reasons he cared about her.

She was a fighter, willing to take a risk if she had to. More and more he thought of what it would be like to have a strong woman like Macy standing beside him, facing whatever life threw at them. Two hearts bound together by the kind of love his father and mother had shared, raising a family together. Was that in their future? Or was it an impossible dream?

Macy interrupted his musing with a question. "Seriously, Nick, who do you think could have killed my mother?"

He puffed out a breath of air. "I don't know, but I'm beginning to think it might not have anything to do with your father. It might have been someone with a grudge toward Megan. Have you learned the name of anyone who might have had something against her?"

"No, but there's something else you don't know. I had another phone call. He said that two women had died in this house. I would be the third."

Nick's blood ran cold. She would be the third? He wanted to get her out of here, but he knew it would be a waste of time to try to persuade her, and she wouldn't let him stay. He knew better than to ask. She was obsessed with learning the secrets of this house, thinking it held the key to her mother's death, and maybe she was right. Regaining her memory could be their best chance to find the killer. If only it wasn't so dangerous. He pulled his attention back to Macy.

"He said two women had died? He must have meant Opal and Megan."

"Which makes me wonder about my grandmother Lassiter. Was there anything suspicious about her death?"

Nick shook his head, trying to think. "Not that I know, but it's something to look into."

"Will you check into it?"

"I sure will. And I'll talk to Sam and see where we go from here. Talk to her doctor, see what he has to say. I'll get on it right now." At least he had something to work on. But if there had been anything suspicious, why hadn't anyone said so? He remembered what Hilda had said, that Opal had changed. She seemed to be thinking someone other than Steve had killed Megan. Had she found something that had pointed to a killer? If so, had she been murdered, too?

"What about an autopsy? Would that help?" Macy asked.

"Not really. After a body has been embalmed, unless there's an obvious reason for the cause of death, like a gunshot it might not show what we need to know."

"Well, it was just a thought," Macy said. "But if it won't work, then it would be an expensive waste of time."

Nick got to his feet and she stood to face him. Almost automatically he reached out for her. She took a step toward him, and he caught her in his arms, pulling her against him. She was so warm, so alive. He had to keep her that way. The thought of her being here alone, of anything happening to her, made him sick to his stomach.

She raised her face to look at him, and his lips met hers, soft, tender, so sweet. He held her closer, hating to let her go. Nick felt a surge of emotion, so strange and sweet it almost overwhelmed him. Macy. She'd walked into his life and changed it in ways he had never imagined would happen. She snuggled closer and their lips met again. He wanted to stay here with her but there were things he needed to do, people he wanted to talk to.

He'd kissed other women, had dated some, but no one had gotten close to him the way Macy had. And now that he'd fallen in love with Macy, he was in danger of losing her. He couldn't let that happen. Someone out there had to have the information he needed, and he was going to find it before anything else happened.

Before anything happened to the woman he loved.

Macy followed Nick to the door, her lips still warm from his kiss. She couldn't deny it any longer. She was in love with Nick Baldwin, but he hadn't mentioned love, and she didn't want to be the first to say it. Besides, she was in danger. She had to distance herself from him until this was settled. She couldn't bear it if she caused anything to happen to Nick.

She closed the door behind him and turned, intending to walk back to the living room. Suddenly she stopped in her tracks. A blinding flash of memory hit her like a hammer blow. Childish laughter, a young voice crying out, "Again. Swing me higher, Daddy."

Macy slumped down to the bottom stair, tears flooding her eyes as the memory rose from deep inside her. It had been so strong, so compelling, she could almost believe she had actually heard it.

She had run to her father and he had picked her up, swinging her high in the air. She had felt so safe, so... loved. If she never learned anything else, living in this house was giving her back her father and mother.

She was beginning to remember.

Macy believed with all her heart God was helping her recall her life in this house. He'd help her remember her mother's killer, too. He would help her recall that fatal night and the name of the monster who had crept into this house, bent on destroying her family.

That night, she decided for the first time to sleep in the child's room, in the bed where she slept when she lived here. At first she had trouble going to sleep, but eventually weariness overcame her.

Voices.

Shouting.

It's your fault. You brought this on yourself. A voice filled with hatred. The sound of something being over- turned.

Macy woke to find herself halfway down the stairs. She gripped the banister, staring down at the place where she had been found unconscious with a fireplace poker lying beside her. Sinking down to sit on the step, she wiped at the tears cascading down her cheeks. That was why she had come downstairs that night. She had heard the voices, the shouting, the horrible sounds of her mother's death. She'd tried to stop it, had run toward the living room, but there the memory stopped, short of letting her see her mother's killer.

Why, God? Why can't I see what happened? Help me, please.

She knew she had come one step closer, but would she take that final step—remember what happened that night before the killer could strike again? She had a feel- ing someone was plotting to enact the scene once more.

And this time, she would lose more than just her memories.

SIXTEEN

Macy was in her father's office going through a box of papers she had found in an upstairs closet. So far she hadn't discovered anything important, but at least she was getting a better idea of her parents and their lives from the little information she had been able to gather.

The doorbell rang and Macy got up to answer. She opened the door to find Anita Miles standing there. For an instant she wanted to slam the door and walk away. As hateful as this woman was, Macy didn't even want her in the house. But common sense won the battle. Find out what Anita wanted first. But she wasn't up to faking a smile or acting nice.

"Yes?"

Anita gave her a hard stare. "I want to talk to you."

"Fine. Talk."

Anita shook her head. "Not standing out here. I'm coming inside, so get out of my way."

Macy gave her an incredulous stare. Get out of her way? This woman needed a book on manners. "Who do you think you *are*, talking to me like that? This is my home, and you don't come in unless you can behave."

Anita hesitated, then shrugged. "All right. I guess I

came on a bit strong. I want to talk to you. May I come inside and the two of us sit down and discuss it like adults?"

"Well, that's a little better, but not much." Macy stepped back and let her enter. "Go into the living room. It's the first door on the right."

Macy followed, watching as Anita looked around as though she was taking inventory. She stopped in front of the fireplace, looking at the pictures on the mantel. Macy, totally fed up with her behavior, sat down in one of the gold brocade chairs and pointed to the other. "Sit down and speak your piece, then get out. I don't want you here."

"Oh, I'm sure you don't," Anita sneered. "You don't want to accept the truth about your father. I don't blame you. He wasn't anything to be proud of."

Macy shot to her feet. "I've heard from a few people who believe you deliberately lied about him at the trial because he wouldn't have anything to do with you. I can see why. He had better taste than that."

Anita's eyes narrowed and her face flushed. "Better taste? That from Megan Douglas's kid? If I didn't know better, I'd think it was her talking. Like mother like daughter. And neither one worth worrying about."

Macy pointed toward the door. "Get out of here and don't come back."

Anita leaned back in the chair, smiling smugly. "I don't think so. Not until I say what I came to say, and then when I'm ready, I'll leave."

Macy stood by the fireplace, hands on her hips. "Then say it, and get it over with."

"I had a visit from Nick Baldwin the other day. It

seems you've pointed suspicion in my direction. I want you to call off the cops, and do it now."

"What makes you think I have any control over the police? I had no idea he had been to see you. What did he want?"

"He insinuated that I might have something to do with Megan's death. As if I'd dirty my hands on her."

Macy took a step toward her. "That's enough. You leave now."

"Are you going to make me?"

"Are you ready to find out?" Macy stepped closer. "Are you the one who beat my mother to death and hit me in the head with a poker? If so, I want you out of this house. You want to leave while you can, or do you want me to call the police?"

Anita looked at her for a minute then got up. "All right, I'll leave. But this isn't over. And I see you have Neva Miller working for you. She's had an interesting life. Get her to tell you about it sometime."

She walked toward the door and Macy followed, wanting to make sure she actually left. After closing and locking the door behind Anita, Macy returned to the office, feeling a little ashamed of herself. Yes, Anita had it coming, but that didn't give *her* the right to behave like that. *God, help me to control my temper and my mouth.* And that wasn't the first time she'd had to pray that prayer. Still, she felt a perverse enjoyment remembering the look on Anita's face at the idea of someone actually daring to confront her.

The phone rang and she jerked around to stare at it, not wanting to answer. No one had called to threaten her lately, but the phone had rung several times where no one said anything. Just silence, heavy breathing and then the sound of someone hanging up. She walked slowly to pick up the receiver. "Hello?"

No answer. She tried again. "Hello?"

Nothing.

"Who are you? Why are you doing this?"

Silence. Then a mocking laugh, followed by a click. Ending the call.

Nick stopped by, and it was great to see him get out of his patrol car and saunter toward the house. It was so good to be back on a friendly basis with him. From the casual way he was moving, Macy suspected nothing had happened to upset him. He approached the house looking so strong and capable it made her feel safe, just watching him. Having Nick in her life was one of God's greatest blessings.

Nick climbed the steps and sat down, smiling at her. "You doing okay?"

"I guess. How about you?" She was even better now that he'd arrived. Just looking at him set her pulse racing. Sometimes it felt as if she hadn't really lived to her full potential before she met Nick. If nothing else came of this venture, she still had the pleasure of getting to know him.

"I'm all right. I talked to Sam and discussed Opal Lassiter with her doctor. Dr. Hill was surprised when she died. He was just treating her for allergies and some mild arthritis. Nothing serious."

"Hilda said almost the same thing. She'd talked to her earlier that night before she went to bed and she seemed to be all right. So maybe she didn't just die, maybe someone killed her, but I really hate to think that. Everyone

I've talked to said she was a good woman. What could anyone have against her?"

"She might have learned something about Megan. If someone helped Opal to die, we owe it to her to learn about it."

"That's the way I feel, but I'm praying it was from natural causes. I really don't want to think someone murdered her, too. I asked Hilda if she told the police how she felt, and she said no, it didn't come up, and she'd never heard any rumors that anything might have been wrong."

"It's kind of far-fetched, but possible I guess," Nick said, but had the police messed up on a second death connected to the Douglas family? "Anything else happen?"

"Anita dropped by, accusing me of sending you to question her. And then Neva warned me that if my father was innocent, someone out there had a reason to shut me up, and if I kept causing trouble I might be lucky to get out of town alive. That I could be painting a big target on my back, just asking someone to come after me."

Every time she repeated that it sent a shiver up her spine. There were too many ways to kill someone. She couldn't be on guard against all of them.

Nick looked troubled. "I hate to think it, but she might be right. Anita's complaints aren't important, but we need to take every precaution to keep you safe."

She held up a hand, stopping him. "If you're leading up to suggesting I stay somewhere else, just where would you suggest I'd be safer? In a motel? You know better. And I'm not about to go to Hilda's, although she's tried to get me to. There's no way I'm going to put her in danger."

She knew Hilda and Nick were right. She should move out of this house, but something seemed to hold her here. If only she could remember what happened that night, remember the killer's face, she could bring this search to a close. She had to try, regardless of the personal cost.

He sighed. "I guess you're right. We don't know who we're looking for, so there's no way to protect you no matter where you are. But you keep the house locked at all times, and keep your cell phone within reach. I'm not sure where this is leading, but I have a hunch we're starting to worry someone." A very dangerous someone.

Nick watched Macy, noticing she had a wariness about her that was new. A tightness to her expression and a sense of vulnerability. The phone call had to have upset her. It worried him, too. Opal Lassiter had been well liked. She was a good woman, kind, hardworking, always ready to help others. He couldn't think of any reason anyone would kill her unless it was related to Megan's murder. Which worried him. The next victim could very well be Macy, the woman who was deliberately running around asking questions and getting people riled up.

Of course, he'd riled a few people, too, but he wasn't worried about himself. All his thoughts were on keeping Macy safe. "Have you learned anything from the transcript of the trial?"

She shook her head. "No, and I've read it several times. It does seem that the evidence against my father was extremely weak."

"Yeah, I caught that. No matter who killed Megan, there was a concentrated effort among people who should have acted differently to convict your father on some rather flimsy so-called evidence. But I think we have to move past that. Yes, they apparently railroaded Steve, but I've about decided that had nothing to do with Megan's actual death."

"I've thought that, too. The attack on my mother seemed personal, as if whoever killed her hated her for some reason. It was too violent to be normal."

"So we find someone who had something against her. I've asked around town, but I haven't found out anything so far. I think it's there, though—we just have to find it."

She looked so alone, so vulnerable, he wanted to wrap her in his arms and keep her safe, but he knew it would take more than that. Somehow he had to find the person who had killed Megan Douglas and tried to frame her husband. Because, like Macy, he had come around to believing Steve really had received a phone call.

"Did I tell you I talked to Garth Nixon?"

Macy shook her head, looking surprised. "No, you didn't. What happened?"

"Not much. I'd heard he was in town that night and I asked him about it."

"He was in town the night my father died? I didn't know that. What did he say?"

"He acted like it wasn't important, but he didn't give me a direct answer, and he was holding a pencil. He gripped it so tight it snapped in two."

The fire started burning in her eyes. "That shows tension. Did he say anything about my parents?"

Nick hesitated. Yes, he had, and it was all hateful. "He claims your father ruined his life with those editorials."

"We knew that. Anything new?"

He shook his head. It wouldn't help if he said anything, and there was no reason to tell Macy what Garth

Nixon had said about her parents. All of which shoved Garth Nixon up the ladder as a suspect as far as Nick was concerned. So far, he seemed to have the best motive for getting rid of Steve Douglas, and he didn't seem to be too fond of Megan, either.

Macy let her frustration show. "Apparently there's not much to point to anyone. I'd think there would be some clues or something to at least give us an idea where to look."

Nick sighed. "Macy, it's been seventeen years. And back then no one tried very hard to find information that would point to anyone else. What was there is gone by now. We're working in the dark for the most part."

"So we might never learn the truth? Is that what you're saying?"

Determination flooded through her. No matter what happened, she would never give up, never stop praying. She believed with all her heart that God had brought her this far. He wouldn't forsake her now.

"No, that's not what I'm saying. We're not going to quit until we solve this thing, for both of our sakes. But it's not going to be easy, so don't get your hopes up that we're getting close to the end. We've got a few names we're considering, but nothing definite yet."

"I know, but what if it's someone we haven't thought about?"

"I've considered that, too. Look, Macy. I make you a promise. I will never give up until we find the real killer. But you need to realize we're after someone who doesn't want to get caught. Someone who will do whatever it takes to stay free. That means you have to be careful. We don't have any real idea who we're after, so you can't take chances, and if you have any information at all, you have to tell me. I'm trying to protect you, but I need your help."

Macy nodded, knowing he was right. "I'll cooperate. And if I learn anything I'll let you know."

"Be sure you do." He pulled her into his arms, his chin resting on the top of her head. Macy clung to him, sending up a swift prayer on his behalf. He was in danger, too. How could she live with herself if the search for her mother's killer cost Nick his life?

SEVENTEEN

Two days later, the phone rang, startlingly loud in the silent house. Macy paused from washing dishes. Should she answer? Probably, but she didn't want to. These taunting phone calls were dragging her down. She slowly picked up the receiver. "Hello?"

Her shoulders slumped in relief when she heard Nick's voice. After the usual greetings, he got to the point. "You doing all right? No more phone calls?"

"Not so far." And maybe she wouldn't get any more. But that was a useless hope. The person calling wasn't about to give up until she left town or was dead.

"I've been thinking, Macy. What caused you to come to Walnut Grove?"

"What do you mean? You know exactly why I came."

"No, I mean, since you couldn't remember your parents, how did you learn about your mother's death and your father's trial?"

"Oh, I see. Well, I found a box my grandmother had kept with all the information about them. Why?"

"I'd like to see it, if you don't mind. Maybe there's something there that might help us."

"I haven't looked at it since that first time, but I did bring it with me. When would you want to see it?" She was through holding back information. It was time to go through those clippings and letters and see if they could throw new light on this case. And who better to go through it all with her than Nick, the man who was trying to help?

"I've got a little time right now. I could be there in a few minutes if that's okay."

Macy hung up the phone and hurried upstairs to check her makeup and change her tan knit top into one more becoming. Yes, she wanted to look good for Nick. When she'd first come here the last thing on her mind was becoming involved with another man. But her relationship with Nick had only grown. She had a feeling God had a hand in it. If so, it was one more blessing He had given her.

Nick arrived and she stood looking at him for a minute, just enjoying the way his shoulders filled out his blue T-shirt. How his dark curls had been tamed to lightly brush his forehead. She wanted to reach out and ruffle them into an unruly mass, the way she'd seen them so many times. He grinned at her as if he knew what she was thinking, and she felt a blush warm her cheeks.

"Come on in. The box is in the kitchen." Where she would sit across the table from him trying to keep her mind on the contents of that box instead of concentrating on Nick.

He sat down and Macy poured them each a cup of coffee, and then slid the metal container closer where he could reach it. She settled into a chair across from him, waiting. Nick looked from her to the box and back again. "Did your grandmother give you this? Or did you find it after she died?"

Macy glanced away from him, fighting for control.

"She was in the hospital…dying. I was with her. I'd been with her day and night since she'd been admitted. She kept looking at me, acting almost frantic, as if there was something she had to say."

She paused, reliving that night. Nick waited, and she swallowed hard and continued. "Finally she managed to say 'box,' then after a pause she sort of gasped, 'the box.' Then she slumped down with her eyes closed and I ran for the door to get help."

Nick reached across the table, grasping her hands. "Are you all right?"

She nodded, gulping on a sob before struggling to go on. "The nurses came running…and in a few minutes it was all over. My grandmother was gone."

"I'm so sorry you had to go through that alone." Nick murmured. "Wasn't there anyone with you?"

Macy shook her head. "No. She had cancer once before, and we fought our way through that, then after a few years it came back, and this time we lost the battle. It took two years of treatment, two years of her gradually failing. During that time people just sort of dropped away, as if they had forgotten about us."

"All of them? No one tried to help you?"

"Oh, at first they rallied around, but then I guess the newness wore off. Anyway, they stopped coming."

She glanced up at him, not wanting to go on, but feeling compelled to. "I was engaged to a man I'd known since we attended high school together. I thought he would be there no matter what happened."

"And he wasn't?"

Macy heaved a sigh. "Two months after we learned my grandmother's cancer had returned, he started dating a woman I had considered my best friend."

"After that, he didn't come around anymore."

Nick watched her, seeing the glitter of tears, the way she gripped her coffee mug. She'd pulled her hands away from his when she started talking about this man. Did she still have feelings for him? He didn't want to think so. The words fell from him, before he thought about it. "I wish I'd been there. I wouldn't have left you like that."

Macy gave him a crooked smile. "No, I don't believe you would have." She pulled her gaze away from his and gestured toward the box. "I guess we'd better get started."

"Oh...yeah. I guess so." He opened the box, glad to have a change in subject. It was getting too emotional in here.

The box was full of papers. He saw newspaper clippings, folded sheets of paper. Hopefully there would be something here that would give them some information. Information that would lead to a killer.

The doorbell rang and Macy got up to answer it. He heard voices and then she entered the kitchen alone. He looked at her, eyebrows raised.

She gave a quick jerk of her shoulders. "Just Neva. It's cleaning day. She'll start upstairs."

One hour and two cups of coffee later Nick was still reading through the papers in the box, taking time to make notes of anything he thought might help. Macy sat at the other side of the table, doing the same thing. Neva walked into the kitchen and nodded at him before opening the doors under the sink and taking out a bottle of glass cleaner.

She glanced toward the table. "What are you doing now?"

Macy explained the box and its contents. "Have you found out anything new?" Neva asked.

Macy shook her head. "Not yet, but it's extremely clear no one worked very hard to find out who was really guilty. I wonder who made that phone call that sent my father out of town so he wouldn't be here to protect my mother?"

Neva leaned on the table, her voice extremely patient. "He lied about getting that phone call. No one called him. He was here, killing Megan. You have to accept that, Macy. Don't let your guilt over not being able to remember them lead you to make a fool of yourself. Your father was convicted by a jury trial. He was found guilty."

"He was convicted by a so-called jury, most of whom hated him for his politics. My father didn't get a fair trial, and I'm going to find the person who committed the crime and framed him, no matter what it takes."

Nick stopped reading to listen. He'd heard this story all over town, but how could anyone be so sure about that phone call or anything else for that matter?

Was Neva one of the citizens who had condemned Macy's father for his political views? If so, why had she continued working for the family? Maybe he needed to do a little snooping around.

Neva shook her head. "Be careful what you stir up, Macy. If you're right, and I'm not saying you are, you could be bringing a pile of trouble down on yourself. You don't want to do that. I might not have agreed with your father, but I thought a lot of your mother, although she could be irritating sometimes, and I loved your grandmother. I'd hate for anything to happen to you."

"I'd hate that, too. Hey, Neva, was there anything suspicious about my grandmother's death?"

Neva paused. "What are you talking about? The whole town knows Opal died in her sleep. What are you trying to stir up now?"

"I'm not trying to stir up anything, I just want to know what happened."

"Well, no one ever hinted that there was something odd about Opal's death. She died peacefully of natural causes. Don't let your imagination run wild, Macy. And don't cause any more trouble than you have to."

"This *is* something I have to do. Can't you understand? I need to know."

"No, I don't understand why you can't accept what happened. And what about your memory?" Neva demanded. "Is it coming back to you? It doesn't seem realistic that you can't remember anything about that night. I know you were young, but after all, you were here in the house when she was killed."

Macy sat silent, as if trying to decide what to say. Apparently this wasn't anything she really wanted to talk about. Finally she said, "I've had a few flashes of things. I think it's coming back. Maybe not all at once, but a little bit at a time. I'm confident I will eventually remember that night and what happened."

"Well, like I've told you, it'll probably be best for you if you don't," Neva said. "Sometimes we're better off not knowing the past. It can get in the way. Life might be easier if none of us could remember what we've had to live through."

Nick sat quietly listening. Sometimes you could learn more by keeping your mouth shut and letting someone else do the talking. He'd learned earlier how Neva's daughter died, in a fiery crash involving another car. There were no survivors. He had to feel sorry for the woman. She'd had a lot to deal with, and losing a daughter that way had to be rough, but he was finding her comments a little abrasive.

Neva abruptly changed the subject, which seemed to surprise Macy. "What are you going to do with Opal's clothes? The Second Time Around Shop accepts donations. The money supports a good cause."

Macy shook her head, looking stubborn again. "I'm not ready for that yet. I want to take my time going through them and see if there's anything I want to keep."

Nick guessed she'd have to go through her parents' things, too. Probably she'd been putting it off. Not wanting to do that just yet. Who could blame her? She had a lot to deal with. Going through her parents' clothes and deciding what to do with them would be traumatic for her. Better to leave that for later. Much later.

Neva frowned. "Why did you come to Walnut Grove, anyway?"

"I told you why. I'm here to find out what happened to my parents. I will never believe my father killed my mother."

"And like I told you, he had a fair trial with a good lawyer and a jury that found him guilty."

Macy paused, looking like that had brought up an angle she hadn't thought about. "Who was on the jury?"

Nick listened with interest. He hadn't thought to ask about that. It was something he should check into.

Neva shoved a chair a little closer to the table. "I don't remember, but the evidence pointed to Steve."

Nick realized they were just going over the same ground and not really accomplishing anything. Which was pretty much the way things had been going since he'd gotten involved in this case.

Macy looked frustrated. "Look, Neva, I understand where you're coming from, but I truly do believe someone falsified the evidence. My father was set up to divert attention from the real murderer."

Neva shook her head. "You need to back off, Macy. If what you're saying is accurate, it just might get you killed."

Nick figured she might be right about that, but the way Neva said it sounded sort of threatening. He wondered if she meant it that way.

Neva returned to her cleaning. Macy glanced at him, her lower lip trembling. "It's like no one cares about the truth. They just want to leave things the way they are, even if a killer walks free."

Nick shook his head. "Not everyone feels that way. In fact, I believe we might be getting closer than we think."

EIGHTEEN

The next afternoon Nick stopped by Clyde's house. This time he was sitting on his front porch, a shaggy black dog sleeping at his feet. The dog raised his head to watch Nick, growling low in his throat.

"Calm down, Smoky," Clyde leaned over and touched the dog's head. "This one's all right."

Nick climbed the two steps to the porch floor. "Is he mean?"

"Well, he's never bit anyone yet, but I reckon he might given the right circumstances. He's not too fond of strangers. Anything I can do for you?"

Nick sat down in an old wooden straight-backed chair. "Just wasting time, probably. I'm trying to find out something about Megan Douglas. Who might have hated her enough to kill her."

"Well, that's a tough one. Actually Megan was all right. She kept busy with her house and her family, and she had that dress shop. Didn't leave her much time to get involved in anything."

"Was she as political as Steve?"

Clyde spit over the porch railing. "Not so I could tell. Actually, not many people were as political as Steve. He carried it to extremes sometimes. I guess he was mostly right about Garth, but I couldn't see it at the time. Been better if we had both kind of held back a little and not got so wound up as we did."

"So that leaves us with the personal angle. Can you think of anything that would help us there?"

Clyde looked thoughtful. "Well, of course, there's Anita. She's a good hater. I'm not suggesting she killed anyone, but she's got a temper. And someone beat Megan up pretty bad."

"She's on my list. Anyone else?"

"Not right offhand. I'll let you know if something occurs to me. I always figured someone saw Steve's car was gone and broke in looking for money. We had some drug problems back then, too, particularly Raleigh Benson's boy. He kept us hopping."

The Benson boy again. Could he have broken in and found Megan at home? Raleigh would have covered for him, you could bet on that. Nick stood up. "Well, I guess that's all. Thanks for your help."

Clyde leaned back in his chair. "I didn't do all that much, but if there's anything I can do for you, just let me know. One more thing. I hear Neva Miller is cleaning house for Macy. She cleaned for Opal, too. Always wondered why. Megan fired Neva's daughter, Lindy, for stealing. She went to prison and when she got out no one would give her a job. Neva blamed Megan and quit working for her. And then Lindy was killed in that car wreck. Neva pretty much fell apart over that. Went kind of crazy. I guess she's all right now, though."

"She cleans the police station and I've never seen anything out of the way." And he hadn't thought about that. She cleaned at night. Could she have taken the Douglas file? They were used to her, and no one paid much attention. She could have taken it easily enough.

"I might be worrying over nothing, then. Just ignore it," Clyde said.

Nick got in his car and sat for a minute, thinking. Neva's name kept cropping up. She had motive, and she had the opportunity. Neva worked for Macy. Maybe he should drop by Macy's. For some reason he felt a sense of urgency, as if he needed to get over there right now. Maybe it was this feeling he had that someone was closing in on them—that he was running out of time.

Macy had spent a restless night. Still awake at five, she ate an early breakfast and decided to check out her grandmother's room one more time. She went through the closet first, searching pockets in jackets, looking at the top shelf again, to make sure she hadn't missed something important. Not finding anything helpful she sat down in front of the dresser, pulling out the drawers and going through them. Each one held undergarments, gowns, odds and ends, the sort of thing she would expect to find, but the drawers looked tumbled, as if someone had already dug through them. She'd taken a look earlier when she first started searching, but no way had she left it like this.

Someone else had been going through her grandmother's things.

Had Neva been digging through the drawers looking for the diary and left them in this mess? Had she found it and not bothered to mention it? Surely she would have said something if she had. Or would she? You couldn't tell with Neva.

Macy got down on her knees, looking under the bed,

and discovered a few dust bunnies, but nothing else. Odd that Neva hadn't cleaned in here the way she did the other rooms. Macy had noticed it before but dismissed it, believing it was hard for her to spend much time in here since Opal had been her friend. Now she wasn't so sure. There was something almost contemptuous in the way she was letting this room go. As if she did it intentionally. Like maybe she had a reason for not taking care of it.

She turned back the bedspread and discovered sheets and pillowcases still in place looking rumpled, as if they had been slept on. Apparently it hadn't been changed since her grandmother had died. Something she had overlooked earlier, just noticing the bedspread was in place, and not bothering to look underneath it. She needed to have a talk with Neva. If she was going to clean this house, she had to do a better job than this.

Macy pulled off the spread, folded it neatly and placed it in a chair. The sheets came next, and the pillow cases. The mattress was crooked, and she grabbed one corner and shoved it back toward the wall. There was a soft thump, as if something had fallen.

She walked around the end of the bed to stare down at the floor. A tan vinyl-covered book lay there. Curious, she picked it up and thumbed through the pages. A diary.

Her mother's diary. She had found it.

She clutched the book to her chest, and rushed from the room. Downstairs, she fixed a glass of ice water and sat down at the table. Macy slid her hand over the cover, caressing it, and then opened it to the first page. Megan Douglas. Her mother's name.

Reverently she turned the pages, reading slowly, thrilling to the chronicle of her mother's life. One entry caught her eye. *Today Macy took her first steps.* And her mother had thought it was important enough to enter it in her diary. Tears burned her eyes. This book would help her recover her mother. From reading this she would gain knowledge of their life together.

She read slowly, savoring every word. Megan Douglas came alive on the pages of her journal. Macy learned about things the two of them had done together, and about her father. Most of it, though, was about Megan and her thoughts, the way she felt, things she had done. There was quite a bit about the business she had started, and the difficulties of getting good help.

One entry close to the back caught her eye. *I had to fire Lindy today. She's been stealing merchandise. I suspected her but there was no proof, then today she messed up. She took money out of the register and I saw her. She's never been a good worker, more trouble than she's worth. Today was the last straw.*

So her mother had to fire someone. Lindy? The name sounded so familiar, but the sudden sound of the front door opening interrupted her thoughts.

She heard footsteps crossing the foyer. That door had been locked. She always kept it that way. Macy rose to her feet as Neva entered the kitchen.

They stood facing each other, but Neva didn't speak, just stood there, wearing a wooden expression. Macy stared at her, bewildered. "How did you get in?"

Neva shrugged. "Did you really think I was fool enough not to make a copy of the key when I had the chance?"

Macy stared at her, caught by the harsh note in her voice. She'd made a key, knowing she wasn't supposed to have one. And what was she doing here? It wasn't her day to clean, so what was going on?

Neva nodded toward the diary. "What's that you've got?

Macy glanced down at the book and answered, trying not to show any concern, but her mind was racing. "It's my mother's diary. I found it in Grandma Lassiter's room."

"I looked there. Where did you find it?"

"It was between the mattress and the box springs. I was stripping the bed and it fell out."

Neva's lips puckered. "It's been there all this time. Who would have suspected it?"

Macy had about had it with this woman—with her temper, her insistence on having a key, the way she kept popping in without warning, the way she was acting now, as if she was angry about something. It was time she learned who was in charge here. "I guess you should have cleaned the room a little better."

Neva flushed. "If you have any complaint about my cleaning, spit it out."

"You cleaned every room except that one, but the drawers looked like someone had pawed through them. Was it you?"

"Why should I clean the room of a woman who treated me like dirt? I didn't have any use for Opal Lassiter, and I don't care who knows it."

"You said you loved her."

"That was for your benefit. It wouldn't have fit my purpose to tell you the truth."

Macy squinted at her, wondering where this was going. "And what was your purpose?"

"Finding that diary, of course. I couldn't let anyone else find it. And now *you've* got it."

Oh. "You were the one trying to break in?"

Anger glinted in Neva's eyes. "I shouldn't have had to 'break in,' as you put it. I had a right to come in. I cleaned this place, while those two acted like they were too good to do any work. And then Megan destroyed my daughter's life—destroyed me. Megan asked for everything that happened to her. It was her own fault."

Macy's eyes were drawn back to the book. What was there in the diary implicating Neva? She glanced at the next entry.

Neva came into the store today. She jerked things off the hangers, threw them on the floor and stomped on them. I'm halfway afraid of her. She doesn't act like she's sane. She blames me because Lindy went to prison, and now that her daughter's out and back in town, no one will hire her. That's not my fault. Who would want to hire someone who did time for stealing from her employer?

Macy stared at the entry, playing for time. Of course. Lindy was Neva's daughter. And Lindy had worked for Macy's mother.

A new memory kicked in. That blonde in the group picture—that was Lindy. And Lindy hadn't liked her, had teased her. More important, her mother was afraid of Neva. Macy stared at Neva, seeing her differently— seeing her the way she'd seen her that night. As a heartless killer.

She remembered now. Remembered Neva standing over her mother's body, the poker in her hand. Remembered running from this woman. She'd reached the foot of the stairs before the poker must have caused her to black out.

Her expression must have given her away because Neva's eyes sharpened. She strode from the room, returning with the fireplace poker—the very same poker she had used that night.

Now she bounced it against her hand, eyes narrowed, her lips tight. "You won't let it alone, will you? I gave you chance after chance to leave, but no, you wouldn't go, you were on a *mission*."

The word *mission* held a wealth of sarcasm.

Macy licked her lips, trying to think of what to do. "I owed it to them to find out what really happened."

"You owed them nothing. It was just you, full of yourself, trying to succeed where the police had failed. You always were a *brat*. Spoiled rotten. You had to come downstairs that night, didn't you? Couldn't stay up in your room where you belonged. Then you tried to get away from me. I should have hit you harder back then. I'll do a better job this time."

Macy's heart was pounding so hard it made her dizzy. She wanted to do something—anything, but her legs felt like rubber, unable to hold her. Just like all those years ago.

She tried to sound as though she was in control, but her voice shook. "You killed her. Why? What did she ever do to you?"

"What did she do? She fired my daughter. Claimed she was stealing. Had her arrested, even got her sent to prison. How do you think that made me feel? My only child in prison—and there wasn't a thing I could do about it."

"Lindy was a thief."

Neva shook the poker at her. "Don't you dare call her that. Lindy never took anything she didn't need. Megan had it all. She could have shared, but she thought she was better than my daughter—better than me. Just like Opal. *She* thought she was something special, too."

Macy couldn't believe it. Her chest felt so tight she had trouble breathing. How she had been fooled so completely? She had accepted Neva, felt sorry for her. There had been signs, but she'd ignored them. She could see now that it was too late.

She forced out the words past lips gone numb with shock. "You killed her, too."

Neva nodded, smiling widely, eyes overly bright, as if extremely proud of what she had done. "She'd found that diary. I knew something was wrong. She was acting funny. Then she called me that night. Told me not to come back to this house. She was going to tell the police, have me arrested.

"She was old and asleep. No match for *me*. All it took was a pillow. I guess she forgot I had a key. I should have hung on to it. Then I wouldn't have had such a hard time getting in."

Her expression changed from triumph to a cold anger. "But *you*. You couldn't let it rest. Everyone had forgot about it until you came along, getting them all riled up again. Well, you're not as important as you think you are. You're just a problem I have to take care of, the way I took care of Megan and Opal. They were no match for me, and you won't be, either."

If only Nick would show up right now. She needed him. Needed help. *God? Are You there? Help me defend myself against this woman.*

"Don't do this, Neva. You won't get away with it— your car's out front. You'll get caught."

Neva's lips curved back in a wide smile, looking

weirdly excited, as if she couldn't wait to use the poker again. Macy shivered, trying to swallow her fear. Gone was the pleasant-faced woman who just seemed a little odd. Neva's eyes had a wild look. It wouldn't take much to send her spinning out of control. Her mother's written words came back to her. *She doesn't act sane.* Macy took a deep breath, her mind racing. Somehow she had to get out of here. Get outside and call for help. *Father, help me! Please...don't let her kill me, too.*

She glanced around, searching for a weapon. All she had was a glass of ice water, which wouldn't be much against a poker. Neva strode toward her, poker held with both hands, the way a ball player would hold a bat. Macy picked up the glass and stepped away from the table. Neva was almost in striking range. She had to do something...fast. She threw the glass of water, hitting Neva in the face. Ice cubes bounced off her head, striking the floor. She howled with rage, but kept coming.

Macy grabbed a chair, swinging it around between them. The poker connected with the chair in a resounding *whack*. A leg splintered. Neva swung again and Macy jumped back out of range. She glanced frantically around the room, searching for another weapon, but finding nothing.

Macy threw the chair at Neva, catching her midstride. She staggered from the force of the blow. Her foot came down on an ice cube. She slipped, dropping the poker and grabbing the edge of the table for support.

Macy whirled, running for the front door. Neva recovered and was coming after her. She fumbled with the lock, her hands numb with fear. Desperate, she yanked the door open and scrambled out onto the porch. She had an impression of a car pulling into the driveway, heard a voice calling her name, but she didn't have time to look. Not with Neva bursting out of the door right behind her, poker raised high.

Nick ran up the driveway, pulse pounding. Neva. Holding a poker, the type of weapon that had been used to kill Megan Douglas. Holding it as if she meant business. Macy had plunged out the door, apparently trying to get away, but Neva was too close behind her. She'd never make it down the porch steps. He had to get there in time.

Macy turned to face Neva and Nick tried to run faster. Neva lifted the poker, poised to strike. He yelled at her. "Stop! Police!"

Neva paused, giving him a hasty glance. Nick put on a burst of speed. He was almost to the porch steps. *Please, God! Let me get there in time.*

Neva had the poker drawn back again, ready to swing it, her expression so wild she looked almost inhuman. For a moment she seemed startled, glancing toward the driveway. Macy leaped at her, grabbing for the poker. Neva shoved her away. Nick reached the porch steps as Macy grabbed a clay flowerpot holding a ruffled pink begonia.

He dashed up the steps as she drew her arm back and seemed to throw the pot with all the force she could summon. It crashed against the door frame, but not before grazing Neva's head.

Nick dashed past Macy to tackle a disoriented Neva. They crashed to the porch floor and he surged to his feet, reaching for his handcuffs.

As soon as Neva was subdued, he turned his attention to Macy, pulling her into his arms, thanking God she was all right. He'd gotten here just in time.

She looked up and he lowered his head, his lips warm against hers, gentle at first then more demanding. She was safe. Nothing could hurt her now. He'd make sure of that.

When their lips parted, Macy twisted around to look at Neva, lying in a heap on the porch floor. "She killed my mother and my grandmother. Murdered them both."

Nick bent over to pick up the poker, careful not touch it where Neva had gripped. He leaned it against the railing. "She's not going anywhere. I'll call Sam and get some help."

Macy sank into one of the wicker chairs, as if she were unable to stand any longer. Nick watched her as she stared at the woman who had destroyed her family. A woman she had trusted. Neva could have attacked her at any moment when she was working here, catching her completely off guard. Macy had been in danger all this time, and he'd been too slow to realize it. There were others who had seemed more promising. He'd come close to losing Macy, and it would have been his own fault.

Macy glanced at Nick. "I want to hate her, but I'm too numb, too drained of emotion to feel anything."

"You've had a rough time, but it's over now."

"I know, and I also know hating is wrong, but she killed my mother and my grandmother. How can I forgive her?"

"Only with God's help. And I'm here, too. I'll be with you."

Nick sat down close to her, holding her hand until Sam arrived with a couple of other policemen. Then he got to his feet.

Sam climbed the porch steps. "You two all right?"

Macy nodded and attempted a smile, looking as though it took all the strength she had to just acknowledge him.

"We're doing all right," Nick answered. "But it was close."

Sam patted Macy on the shoulder, looking down at her. "I'm sorry it came to this. We should have gotten onto her earlier, but it's over now. You're safe."

He hauled Neva to her feet, eyeing her with obvious contempt. "I've got a cell waiting for you. Let's get going."

He took her by the shoulder, but she jerked away, spitting at him. Sam wiped the spittle off and glared at her. "There'll be no more of that. Now you get down those porch steps and start walking."

He helped her down the steps and started leading her toward the car, but she jerked away again, whirling to face Macy. "You worthless brat! I should have killed you back when I had the chance."

Macy flinched and Nick put his arm around her. "It's all right. She can't hurt you. I won't let her."

Sam propelled Neva down the walk and shoved her into the police car. Nick watched him drive away. What a trail of blood that woman had left behind her, and it wasn't over. They'd still have the trial to get through.

Nick looked down at Macy. "Are you all right?"

She nodded, knowing she wasn't. The way she felt right now, she might never be all right again. "I think so. She tried to kill me."

"Yeah, I saw that. What happened?"

Macy stopped to think, trying to clear her head. "I

found my mother's diary. In it she said she was afraid of Neva, that she wasn't quite sane. Then Neva came in. I'd locked the door, but she had a copy of the key."

She stopped, struggling for control. "Oh, Nick, she said she should have hit me harder that night. I was just seven years old. And she killed my mother."

He pulled Macy to her feet, holding her close and kissing her forehead. "It's over. You're safe and she'll never hurt anyone again."

A car door slammed and Hilda dashed toward the porch. "Macy, are you all right? I just saw the police leading Neva into the station. What happened?"

Macy turned to face her. With Nick's arm around her, holding her close against his side, she could say the words. "She killed my mother and grandmother, and she tried to kill me."

Hilda sagged, holding on to the porch railing. "*Neva?* It was *Neva*? I suspected Anita."

"I suspected several others," Nick said, "but I finally realized she had to be the one."

He looked down at Macy. "I have to go, but I'll be back later. Hilda, you stay with her, okay?"

"Of course. I'll stay as long as she needs me."

Macy watched as he hurried to his police car. He'd be back. He'd said he would be, and Nick Baldwin kept his promises. And when he returned, she'd have so much to tell him.

Hilda took her arm. "Let's go inside. It's quieter there."

Macy looked around. Neighbors were standing on their porches, staring at her. She turned and walked inside, knowing she didn't have to be afraid anymore. God had answered her prayers.

An hour passed, Hilda had gone home, and Nick had returned. He and Macy were sitting in the wicker love seat on the porch. The police had found the device Neva had used to change her voice on the phone. The blonde in the group picture had been Lindy, and Neva had stolen the photo while Macy wasn't looking.

The night air was cool and fresh. Silence closed around them, a blessed relief from all that had happened. Macy took a deep breath, feeling free for the first time since arriving in Walnut Grove.

Nick took her hand. "What are you going to do now?"

Macy hesitated, searching for the words. "I don't know. This house... I've been afraid of it ever since I moved in. Now, it's like a shadow has lifted, as if it's just a normal house, the way it once was."

"So are you planning on living here?

Macy nodded. "I think so. I'd like to see it come alive again, filled with laughter and the sound of voices, and children playing. The way it used to be before all of this happened."

"Would you need any help with that?"

She glanced at him, the corners of her lips quirking in the beginning of a smile. "I'm sure I would. It would take two to make that dream come true."

He brushed the hair off her forehead. "If you're taking applications, I'd like to submit mine."

Macy let the smile blossom as she met his eyes. "I hoped you would. In fact, I was sort of planning on it."

"Oh, Macy." He stood up, pulling her with him, his arms warm and comforting around her. "I love you so much I want to keep you beside me for the rest of my life."

She grinned up at him. "Is that a proposal?"

"I meant it that way. Are you interested?"

"I thought you'd never ask."

He drew her to him, and she saw the love glowing in his eyes. She'd come back to this house, searching for something that had been stolen from her. Now, she not only remembered her life here—remembered her family—but with God's help she and Nick had cleared her father's name and brought her mother's killer to justice.

She stood sheltered in Nick's embrace, so close she could feel his heartbeat. His lips touched hers, tender, loving, and she yielded herself to his kiss. After all her searching for the truth, all the doubts and fears, she was safe, sheltered in the arms of the man she loved with all her heart. Even the house seemed to be smiling.

Macy was home.

* * * * *

Dear Reader,

Thank you for reading *Dangerous Inheritance*. After her grandmother died, Macy Douglas found a box of letters and newspaper clippings and was surprised to learn her mother had been brutally killed, her father had been convicted of the murder and he'd died in prison.

Life is full of surprises, some good, some bad and some them change our lives forever. I've had several surprises, some I enjoyed, some I didn't. I'm sure you have, too.

Macy, with Nick's help, learns to put her trust in God. It's been a struggle, but over the years I've learned to put my problems in God's hands and leave them there. He's always quick to answer our prayers and help us through the most trying times—a never-ending source of peace and comfort.

May God be with you always, through both the good times and the bad.

Barbara Warren

REQUEST YOUR FREE BOOKS!

2 FREE RIVETING INSPIRATIONAL NOVELS
PLUS 2 FREE MYSTERY GIFTS

Love Inspired®
SUSPENSE

Love the Love Inspired book you just read?

Your opinion matters.

Review this book on your favorite book site, review site, blog or your own social media properties and share your opinion with other readers!